YORK NOTES

General Editors: Professor A.N. Jeffares (*University of Stirling*) & Professor Suheil Bushrui (*American University of Beirut*)

Charles Dickens

BLEAK HOUSE

Notes by J. J. Simon

DOCTEUR EN PHILOSOPHIE ET LETTRES (LUXEMBOURG)
Lecturer, Cours Universitaires de Luxembourg

LONGMAN
YORK PRESS

YORK PRESS
Immeuble Esseily, Place Riad Solh, Beirut

ADDISON WESLEY LONGMAN LIMITED
Edinburgh Gate, Harlow,
Essex CM20 2JE, England
Associated companies, branches and representatives
throughout the world

First published 1982
Tenth impression 1996

ISBN 0-582-03093-5

Produced by Longman Singapore Publishers Pte Ltd
Printed in Singapore

Contents

Contents

Part 1

Introduction

N<small>O OTHER</small> E<small>NGLISH</small> A<small>UTHOR</small>, with the exception of Shakespeare, has created such a host of characters, memorable both in England and abroad, as Charles Dickens. Almost all his novels have been, and still are, best sellers. The adjective 'Dickensian' is part of the English language, and his work has become a permanent part of English civilisation. If Dickens had a period of decline with literary critics, there is a new interest in his work in our age through sympathy with the increasing pessimism in his later novels.

Bleak House (1853) is Dickens's first successful effort to integrate a gallery of characters from all classes, a long list of social and political problems, and a fascinating multitude of memorable visual details, into one single view of society.

The year 1851 (in which Dickens began writing *Bleak House*) was the year of the Great Exhibition, a spectacular statement of the achievements of the age; but it was also a period in which many a negative diagnosis of mid-Victorian England was made. Dickens certainly agreed with the more sombre analysts of his time, and tried to translate their diagnosis into his own language.

Life of Charles Dickens

Charles Dickens was born in Landport, now part of Portsmouth, a naval port on the south coast of England on 7 February 1812. He was the second child and eldest son of the eight children of John and Elizabeth Dickens. John Dickens, a clerk in the Naval Pay Office, was a lively, kind-hearted man; he was rarely able to live within his income. Charles's mother was born Elizabeth Barrow, daughter of Charles Barrow, a Chief Conductor of Money for the Navy Board. Mr Micawber, in *David Copperfield*, and Mrs Nickleby, in *Nicholas Nickleby*, are to some extent portraits of Dickens's parents.

Young Charles spent his early years in Portsmouth and London. In 1817 his father was transferred to Chatham, and the family lived there until 1823. For Charles these must have been the happiest childhood years. Much later, at the zenith of his fame, he bought a house at Gad's Hill which he had already admired as a boy.

When John Dickens was recalled to London in 1823 he left Chatham in debt. A friend of the family who had an interest in a blacking warehouse at Hungerford Stairs offered Charles work. Although children's work was common enough at that time, Charles Dickens never really recovered from this humiliating experience. It was, according to Dickens, as if his father had clean forgotten that his son had any claim to be educated.

Only a few days after Charles had started labelling bottles for six shillings a week, his father was arrested for debt and sent to the Marshalsea Debtors' Prison, where his whole family joined him, except for Charles, who had found a room nearby. Thanks to a legacy from John Dickens's mother the family was able to leave the Marshalsea and settled in a small house in Somers Town, though Mrs Dickens still insisted on Charles's working at the blacking factory. 'I never shall forget, I never can forget, that my mother was warm for my being sent back'.

His father eventually took him away and for the next two and a half years Charles attended Wellington House Academy, a school with an excellent reputation. In 1827 he started work as an office boy with Ellis and Blackmore, a firm of solicitors in Raymond Buildings, overlooking Holborn.

Although Dickens found law a dull business, he was to absorb much of its atmosphere and background and immediately had an eye for odd characters. His father having learnt shorthand, Charles followed his example and, at almost seventeen, started a career as a freelance reporter at Doctors' Commons.

In 1829 he met Maria Beadnell, a banker's daughter, and fell hopelessly in love. A born actor, Dickens also developed a keen interest in the stage, though he mainly worked for the *Mirror of Parliament*, the *True Sun* and finally the *Morning Chronicle*, a liberal daily.

In 1833 his first sketch, *A Dinner in Poplar Walk*, was published in the *Monthly Magazine*. Dickens's career as a writer had begun, and in 1836 two volumes, *Sketches by Boz*, illustrated by the well-known artist George Cruikshank, were published by Macrose. The same year, in April, Dickens married Catherine Hogarth, the daughter of a fellow journalist, having put a sudden stop to his long and tantalising courtship of Maria Beadnell. Years later, his descriptions of the characters of Estella in *Great Expectations* and Flora Casby in *Little Dorrit* were influenced by his relationship with Maria Beadnell.

Dickens was now lucky to be offered a commission by a new firm of publishers, Chapman and Hall, who were looking for a writer willing to describe a then familiar theme, sporting incidents, that were to be illustrated by a popular artist, Seymour. Dickens agreed and thus Pickwick was born. Though not immediately a success, *Pickwick Papers* (1836–7) became extraordinarily popular, the success being partly due to the method of publishing by instalments, but also to its new illustrator

Hablôt Browne (Phiz), and to one character, Sam Weller. The enthusiastic reception of *Pickwick Papers* made Dickens leave the *Morning Chronicle* and he immediately embarked on writing a new novel (*Oliver Twist*, 1838), to be followed by a third success, *Nicholas Nickleby* (1838–9).

The shock of the unexpected death of his sister-in-law Mary Hogarth and problems with his publishers made the help of John Foster, who was to become his first biographer, all the more precious during this period. He also came to know Leigh Hunt (1784–1859) and Walter Savage Landor (1775–1864), who were caricatured as Skimpole and Boythorn in *Bleak House*, and, among many others, Thomas Carlyle (1795–1881), whose work and style deeply influenced him. The publication of *The Old Curiosity Shop* (1840) and *Barnaby Rudge* (1841) completes what may be called the first group of Dickens's novels.

Dickens's fame abroad, especially in America and Russia, was already enormous by then and early in 1842 he and his wife set off for the United States. He was, of course, eager to come to know what he thought was a truly democratic society; he wanted to meet American writers, such as Washington Irving (1783–1859), and he was keen to discuss the problems of copyright protection. Dickens's often negative impressions were recorded in *American Notes* (1842), which attracted little notice in England. *Martin Chuzzlewit* (1843–4) was selling badly, although the character of Mrs Gamp in that novel was an immediate success. This was followed by the extremely successful *A Christmas Carol* (1843).

After a spell of travelling that brought him to Italy, Switzerland and France, Dickens published *Pictures from Italy* (1846) and began editing the *Daily News*. For the next two years he worked on *Dombey and Son*, a novel with a much more carefully elaborated plot than anything he had written before.

David Copperfield (1849–50), in which his own childhood is explored, was held to be his masterpiece. It is a novel that does not belong to any other group of his works. 'I have in my heart of hearts a favourite child. And his name is DAVID COPPERFIELD'.

Dickens's ever present interest in social problems was further manifested in the weeklies *Household Words* and *All the Year Round*, both considerable publishing successes. *Bleak House* (1852–3), *Hard Times* (1854) and *Little Dorrit* (1855–7), all have strong social themes, attacking the 'Law's Delay', schooling and the crippling effects of abuses in government and administration. George Bernard Shaw (1856–1950) declared *Little Dorrit* to be 'a more seditious book than *Das Kapital*'. *Bleak House* was to be the last of the Dickens novels that Hablôt Browne (Phiz) illustrated. Though Phiz successfully illustrated and complemented some of Dickens's best-known novels, his talents do not quite convey the murky atmosphere of some of the scenes he tries to picture.

Relations in the household had become strained, and in 1858 Dickens separated from his wife, the mother of his ten children, a step which was to mar his reputation. He was deeply infatuated with a young actress, Ellen Ternan, and spent most of his time at home in Kent, at Gad's Hill. In the meantime he had taken to giving public readings, a decision which impaired his health quite seriously, as these readings were close to actual stage productions.

In 1859 he published *A Tale of Two Cities* and in 1860–1 *Great Expectations*, which became one of his most popular books. In 1864 *Our Mutual Friend*, his last completed work, appeared. A second visit to America and further public readings, which, though very popular, were exceedingly exhausting, precipitated his physical decline. Dickens died at Gad's Hill on 9 June 1870, leaving his last novel, *The Mystery of Edwin Drood*, unfinished. His remains were buried in Poets' Corner at Westminster Abbey.

A note on law courts and colleges

Whereas the rest of Europe uses the Napoleonic code in law, which took over the tradition of codified Roman Law at the beginning of the nineteenth century, English law is based on precedent, that is, justice is given by making use of the opinions of the judges in previous cases. Furthermore, several kinds of courts existed in England at the time when Dickens wrote *Bleak House* and at the period in which he set his novel.

(1) The Courts of Common Law

These courts dealt with such crimes as theft, robbery or murder. Thus Trooper George is arrested in *Bleak House* by Police Inspector Bucket; he is committed to jail and he would have been tried and sentenced in a common court by a judge and a jury.

When Nemo's body is discovered, a coroner (and an officer of a Court of Common Law) has to lead an inquest, and is assisted by a jury from the locality (see Dickens's description in Chapter 11 and Tulkinghorn's report to Sir Leicester at the end of Chapter 12).

(2) The Court of Chancery

This court settled legacies, wills, trusts or wardships. Such disputes were handled by the Lord Chancellor, the chief judge in England, and a member of the Cabinet. The Court of Chancery dealt with such issues where Common Law failed (in lack of precedent, for instance), and decided on the principles of Equity. The High Court of Chancery was supposed to compensate for fixed rules of Common Law and to protect the individual from any exaggerated rigidity. In Dickens's time it had developed its own system of legalistic technicalities and precedents and had led to obvious abuse.

There was no jury in the Court of Chancery and the presiding judge would reach his verdict after considering written evidence given to him in form of affidavits. Such a document, written by Nemo, arouses Tulkinghorn's suspicions (see Chapter 2). Therefore Miss Flite, Gridley and Richard all go to court to *listen* to the evidence being read. Dickens himself had experienced the frustratingly slow procedures in Chancery as he had had to drop a suit against pirate-printers of *A Christmas Carol*.*

If a will was claimed to be invalid by a would-be inheritor, a solicitor would state that person's (the plaintiff's) claims against his rival's (the defendant's). Once such procedures were initiated, the potential heirs could not benefit from the estates they had inherited until a decision was reached. The estate would be 'in Chancery' and might decay before anyone could inherit it and look after it properly. Thus 'this desirable property [Tom-all-Alone's] is in Chancery, of course' (Chapters 16 and 46).

The people who had filed a suit in Chancery (the litigants) had to pay for all the expenses of their solicitors and witnesses, and these expenses were quite likely to ruin them – hence Dickens's reference to 'mountains of costly nonsense' in the opening chapter and John Jarndyce's comments in Chapter 8, 'it's about nothing but costs ... all the rest has melted away'.

Further delay became inevitable when the question had to be settled as to which of the two courts (Common Law or Chancery) was to have jurisdiction. Therefore John Jarndyce (Chapter 8) says 'Equity sends question to Law, Law sends questions back to Equity; Law finds it can't do this, Equity finds it can't do that ...'

Of course, a lot of cases were correctly settled within a reasonable time, but three cases were well known to Dickens, one for its endless dragging on, another for the expenses involved, the third for both. They were the William Jennings case (which started in 1798 and not yet settled in 1851 when Dickens began writing *Bleak House*) and the Day case (which had opened in 1834 and by 1853 had cost the litigants more than seventy thousand pounds). Dickens mentions the third case in his preface.

The Inns of Court

The word 'inn' may be misleading. It is not synonymous with a pleasant, small hostelry in the country; an Inn of Court 'combined some of the

*See also 'The Chancery Prisoner' in *Pickwick Papers*, Chapter 43.

functions of a law school and a dining-club, with rooms and dining-hall for students and other residents, and usually a chapel'.

An Inn of Court could regulate the exclusive right that qualified a person for admission to the Bar. The buildings included offices for the lawyers. Mr Vholes has such offices in Symond's Inn. The names either refer to their founders (Thavies, Symond) or to their local situation (Middle and Inner Temple occupy ground once belonging to the Knight Templars in the early Middle Ages). In the neighbourhood of these Inns one could find legal stationers and copyists, such as Mr Snagsby or Nemo.

Barristers and solicitors

A future *solicitor* (Conversation Kenge, Carboy, Tulkinghorn) had his training in a lawyer's office. As an articled clerk he was bound to his employer by a contract ('articles'). Having qualified, a solicitor advised his clients on legal matters; he could prepare a case, but did not plead in court. *Barristers* (members of the Bar) presented the case before the judge.

Mr Blowers, 'the eminent silk gown' of the opening chapter of Bleak House, is such a barrister (a barrister's functions were those of an *avocat-avoué* in other countries; a solicitor would come close to a *conseiller juridique*).

Terms and vacation

'London Michaelmas term lately over, and the Lord Chancellor sitting in Lincoln's Inn Hall.' These terms help us to find out about the time it takes the Jarndyce case to draw towards its close. There were four terms: Hilary Term (January 11–31), Easter Term (April 15–May 8), Trinity Term (May 27–June 12), Michaelmas Term (November 2–25). Courts could still be in session between these terms and would change the place of meeting, from, for instance, Westminster Hall to Lincoln's Inn, as in the opening scene of *Bleak House*.

The summer vacation lasted four months and the Inns of Court were only thinly populated then (see Chapters 14 and 20).

Setting

Bleak House. The original of the fictional Bleak House may have been either in Gombard's Road, St. Albans, or off the main St. Albans–Hatfield Road. (Dickens's holiday home at Broadstairs, Fort House, is called Bleak House today. It has no connection with the novel, however.) St. Albans, a cathedral town in Hertfordshire, was a suitable area for the brickmaking industry, because the soil contained a good deal of clay.

Chesney Wold. The original of the Dedlocks' Lincolnshire home was Rockingham Castle in Northamptonshire (a wold is a hilly or rolling region).

London. A visitor to London in the 1840s would have been impressed by the topographical precision of *Bleak House*. Everything, from street names to professions, is enclosed within half a mile of Chancery Lane.

Tom-all-Alone's. These slums have been identified by some as a rookery on the eastern side of Bedfordbury, Strand. They were pulled down in 1880.

Dickens's literary background and other influences

Dickens was a writer of great originality and individuality. In *David Copperfield*, however, the opening chapters of which include autobiographical reminiscences, the reader is informed that young David (alias young Charles Dickens) came to know the works of Tobias Smollett (1721–71), Oliver Goldsmith (1730?–74) and Miguel de Cervantes (1547–1616). He was also familiar with *Tom Jones* (1749), *Gil Blas* (1715–35), *Robinson Crusoe* (1719) and the Shakespearean characters.

The young writer met Thomas Carlyle in London in 1840. Carlyle's style and especially the social message of his writings were to have a lasting influence on him.

Furthermore there is no doubt that Dickens's thorough knowledge of the teeming London world, his experience as a journalist and his interest as well as his active participation in the theatre made him in his earlier work more interested in the nature of characters and the accuracy of detail than in creating a coherent plot.

His later novels, however, show him to be a much more mature writer, deeply troubled by social and political problems, whose journalistic concerns with topics of the day came to help his artistic purposes at least as much as his never flagging, passionate interest in the single human being. The comprehensiveness of his sympathy as well as the maturity of his genius made Dickens write a judgement on his age that is nowhere more coherent than in *Bleak House.*

Bleak House is the second in a series of seven novels (the first being *Dombey and Son*) in which social analysis linked with satire produces works of art with obvious revolutionary implications. Whatever Dickens had witnessed in the London slums, read about in the papers or in the work of fellow-writers or had discussed with the collaborators of the magazine he edited he used now on a higher, symbolic level in his novels, especially in *Bleak House* and *Little Dorrit*. We have only to compare the following two extracts to see how his sensitive recording mind used those materials to create a moral universe:

'The State, left to shape itself by dim pedantries and traditions, without distinctness of conviction, or purpose beyond that of helping itself over the difficulty of the hour, has become, instead of a luminous vitality permeating with its light all provinces of our affairs, a most monstrous agglomerate of inanities, as little adapted for the actual wants of a modern community as the worst citizen need wish. The thing it is doing is by no means the thing we want to have done . . . .

A mighty question indeed! Who shall be Premier, and take in hand the 'rudder of government', otherwise called the 'spigot of taxation'; shall it be the Honourable Felix Parvulus, or the Right Honourable Felicissimus Zero? By our electioneerings and Hansard Debatings, and ever-enduring tempest of jargon that goes on every-where, we manage to settle that; to have it declared, with no bloodshed except insignificant blood from the nose in hustings-time, but with immense beershed and inkshed and explosion of nonsense, which darkens all the air, that the Right Honourable Zero is to be the man. That we firmly settle; Zero, all shivering with rapture and with terror, mounts into the high saddle; cramps himself on, with knees, heels, hands and feet; and the horse gallops – whither it lists. That the Right Honourable Zero should attempt controlling the horse – Alas, alas, he, sticking on with beak and claws, is too happy if the horse will only gallop anywhither, and not throw him. Measure, polity, plan or scheme of public good or evil, is not in the head of Felicissimus; except, if he could but devise it, some measure that would please his horse for the moment, and encourage him to go with softer paces, godward or devilward as it might be, and save Felicissimus's leather, which is fast wearing. This is what we call a Government in England, for nearly two centuries now.'

(Thomas Carlyle, *Latter-Day Pamphlets*, 1850, Nos 3–4.)

Now read this text:

'Her Majesty contemplates with grateful satisfaction and thankful-ness to Almighty God the tranquility which prevails throughout her dominions; together with that peaceful industry and obedience to the laws which insure the welfare of all classes of her subjects. It is the first desire of Her Majesty to promote the advance of every social improvement, and, with the aid of your wisdom, still further to extend the prosperity and happiness of her people'.

(Speech from the Throne on National Progress, 20 August 1853.)

As Dickens informs us in his own preface* he relies on true events concerning the Court of Chancery (including Gridley's case) and he

*See also the author's preface to *Little Dorrit*.

considers the recording of social events an important aspect of novel writing, hence some topics are recurrently represented in *Bleak House*: Government, the law and pollution. Historical scholars have discovered many minor topics of the day convincingly threaded into the tightly woven plot of this novel.*

A note on the text

Bleak House was written in nineteen monthly parts, the last of these being a double number. Dickens began writing it at Tavistock House, his new London home, in November 1852. He completed it in August 1853 at the Château des Moulineaux, which he had rented near Boulogne, in France. The complete manuscript of *Bleak House* is preserved in two volumes in the Forster Collection at the Victoria and Albert Museum in London.

The first edition appeared in two forms with identical texts: the nineteen monthly instalments and the one volume edition published by Bradbury and Evans, London, 1853.

Many editions have since appeared. A useful and easily available modern edition, which has been used in the preparation of these notes, is that published by Penguin Books, Harmondsworth, 1971.

*See John Butt and Kathleen Tillotson, 'The Topicality of *Bleak House*' in *Dickens at Work*, Methuen, London, 1957, pp. 177–200. See also Humphrey House, *The Dickens World* (Oxford Paperbacks No 9), Oxford University Press, Oxford, 1972, pp. 30–31.

Part 2

Summaries
of BLEAK HOUSE

A general summary

In a symbolic opening chapter an all pervading fog covers the country, London and the High Court of Chancery. A hearing of the suit of Jarndyce and Jarndyce, which has been dragging on for years, ruining those people concerned with it, begins the story.

Lady Dedlock, wife of Sir Leicester Dedlock, Baronet, from Lincolnshire, is one of the claimants of that suit. In the Dedlock town house in London she is shown a document by her solicitor Mr. Tulkinghorn, the handwriting of which profoundly upsets her.

Interspersed with the tale told by the omniscient narrator is the story told by Esther Summerson. Illegitimate, she was brought up by a harsh godmother, on whose death she was sent to a boarding school near Reading. This arrangement was made by Mr John Jarndyce of Bleak House, through his legal adviser, Mr Kenge, of Kenge and Carboy's.

Six years later, at the age of twenty, Esther goes to act as a companion to a ward of the Court in the Jarndyce cause, Ada Clare, at Mr Jarndyce's house. Richard Carstone, another ward and Ada's cousin, is also there.

While Richard optimistically waits for a positive end to the Jarndyce suit, his guardian vainly tries to dispel any such illusions. The young people come to know old, mad Miss Flite, another victim of Chancery. She introduces them to Krook, an illiterate and eccentric old rag-and-bottle merchant, who has piles of old Chancery documents at his messy shop. They spend a night in London at the house of Mrs Jellyby, a philanthropist who devotes all her energy to the cause of African natives, thereby grossly neglecting her own family. Ada and Esther accompany Mrs Pardiggle, another example of ineffectual philanthropy, to a poor brickmaker's home near St Albans, where Esther tries to comfort the brickmaker's wife, Jenny, whose baby has just died. Esther covers the baby's face with her handkerchief.

Esther is given the keys of Bleak House by Mr Jarndyce and becomes a perfect housekeeper. At Bleak House she meets Skimpole, 'a mere child', who, though a pleasant talker, sponges on Mr Jarndyce and has a debt paid by Richard.

Mr Guppy, a young clerk at Kenge and Carboy's, has fallen in love with Esther. Travelling through Lincolnshire he visits the Dedlocks' country house. He is struck by a portrait of Lady Dedlock, though at the moment he cannot think whom she reminds him of. Guppy proposes to Esther, who refuses him.

In the meantime Mr Tulkinghorn has made inquiries at Mr Snagsby's (a law stationer's) about the writer of that document that troubled Lady Dedlock so much and he has found out that Krook has a lodger, Nemo, to whom Snagsby gives documents to copy. When Tulkinghorn goes to Nemo's shabby room, he finds him dead, presumably of an overdose of opium. Nemo had no friends except Jo ('Toughey'), a young crossing-sweeper, who gives evidence at the inquest and sweeps the entrance to the repulsive burial-ground where Nemo's remains have been brought. Lady Dedlock affects complete indifference when Tulkinghorn informs her of the results of his investigations.

Ada and Richard have fallen in love and Richard decides to become a surgeon. He is, however, of an unstable disposition, and soon switches over to the law, then to the army. His suspicions (completely ill-founded) are growing that John Jarndyce is at the root of his problems. He is convinced that he will see through the entangled procedures of the law-suit and that he will be a rich man one day.

Esther meets Allan Woodcourt, a young doctor, with whom she falls in love; the feeling is, however, almost drowned by her gratitude towards John Jarndyce.

Jo, who has told Tulkinghorn that he has been given some money by a veiled lady who wanted to be shown Nemo's grave, identifies that lady's clothes in Tulkinghorn's chambers, though he does not recognise the woman who wears them. She is Lady Dedlock's French maid Hortense, who is jealous of Rosa, a young servant girl whom Lady Dedlock prefers, and is now trying to harm her mistress.

Tulkinghorn patiently gathers information about the wife of one of his most important clients, Sir Leicester Dedlock. He also tries to get another piece of writing in Nemo's hand from 'Mr George', a former soldier who turns out to be the runaway son of the Dedlocks' old housekeeper.

Parallel to Tulkinghorn, Guppy has been carrying on his own investigations and he calls on Lady Dedlock. He has found out that Esther's name is not Summerson, but Hawdon, that she is Lady Dedlock's illegitimate daughter, and that Nemo was a pseudonym used by Captain Hawdon. Esther visits Jenny again, together with Charley, a young orphan girl, now her maid. Here she finds Jo, who has a bad fever. They bring him to Bleak House where first Charley, then Esther, catch smallpox from him. The disease leaves Esther badly scarred. While recovering at the house of Mr Boythorn (a friend of John Jarndyce living in Lincolnshire and a neighbour to the Dedlocks) she meets Lady Dedlock during a thunderstorm. Lady Dedlock has guessed identity because of the handkerchief she found at Jenny's hovel. Although she loves her daughter very much, they must not meet again, and their relationship must not be disclosed, as this would mean ruin for both of them.

Guppy, eager to get at Nemo's papers, has a friend lodged in the deceased law-writer's room. They expect Krook to hand them over those papers, but Krook dies of spontaneous combustion. His belongings fall into the hands of his brother-in-law, Grandpa Smallweed.

Tulkinghorn has blackmailed 'Mr George' into giving him a specimen of Captain Hawdon's handwriting. He calls on Lady Dedlock again. He will not betray her secret, provided that she does not change anything in her present situation; above all she must not leave Sir Leicester as she intended to do.

Hortense, Lady Dedlock's French maid, expects Tulkinghorn to find her a new post for all the help she has given him. Tulkinghorn haughtily orders her to leave his house. After one more interview with Lady Dedlock, Tulkinghorn is found shot dead in his chambers. 'Mr George' is arrested for the murder by Inspector Bucket, but anonymous letters accuse Lady Dedlock of the deed. Furthermore a female figure, not unlike her, has been seen around Tulkinghorn's place on the very night of the murder. Guppy tells Lady Dedlock that her story is known by several people (Smallweed, Mr and Mrs Chadband, Mrs Snagsby). Lady Dedlock leaves her home and Sir Leicester charges Inspector Bucket to find her again. Bucket calls for Esther and tries to follow her. They leave London, but they turn back after a while. They have been misled, because Lady Dedlock has managed to change clothes with Jenny. Esther finds her mother dead at the gate of the shabby burial-ground where Captain Hawdon (Nemo) lies.

Richard Carstone has become the helpless victim of Vholes, a selfish solicitor. He has secretly married Ada and is living, ill, haggard and anxious, at Symond's Inn.

The suit in Chancery draws to its close; there will be no lucky heirs. The whole of the estate has been swallowed up in costs. Richard dies, fully conscious of his mistakes and reconciled to John Jarndyce.

John Jarndyce, who had proposed to Esther, gallantly steps down in favour of Allan Woodcourt, who looked after the dying Jo and was a faithful visitor to Richard. Allan will work among poor people in Yorkshire, where John Jarndyce has built him a house, called Bleak House, an exact replica of the old Bleak House, in which Allan and Esther will live. Ada and her baby son, Richard, stay with Mr Jarndyce.

Detailed summaries

Chapter 1: In Chancery

Michaelmas term is over and the Lord Chancellor is sitting in Lincoln's Inn Hall. There is a thick fog and a sooty drizzle outside, darkening everything, as if the snow had 'gone into mourning, for the death of the sun'.

Everyone is engaged in a confused way in cases that are never brought to an end. The case of Jarndyce and Jarndyce is going on, a 'scarecrow of a suit'. Only a man from Shropshire and a little mad old woman (Miss Flite) are present. Both are ruined suitors.

The suit, unwholesome and corrupting, is again postponed, but the Chancellor tells the court he is about to see the young girl and the young man in the case, now waiting in his private rooms, before making out an order to them to reside with their remote cousin.

NOTES AND GLOSSARY:

aits: small islands
Greenwich pensioners: retired soldiers
Chancery: See the notes on law, courts and colleges in Part 1, pp. 8–9
Lincoln's Inn Hall: See pp. 9–10
Temple Bar: archway that led to the old walled city of London. It was removed in 1878
lantern that has no light: louvre, a roof turret with slatted apertures for ventilation
lunatic in every madhouse: Chancery jurisdiction could decide whether a person was to be declared insane
curtained sanctuary: the platform on which the Chancellor sat had curtains on three sides
sallow prisoner: Dickens had protested in an article in *Household Words* in favour of those people who had been committed to prison for contempt
fair wards of court: minors, like Ada and Richard
sharking: swindling
blue bags: lawyers' documents were carried in such bags

Chapter 2: In Fashion

The world of fashion, a muffled and sometimes unhealthy world, is not unlike the Court of Chancery.

Lady Dedlock is in her London house before leaving for Paris; she has come down from her 'place' in Lincolnshire, Chesney Wold, which is now soaked with November rains, boring her to death. She has left it in the care of an old housekeeper. Sir Leicester Dedlock, Baronet, also present, is some twenty years older than his wife, whom he married for love. Sir Leicester is prejudiced, fully convinced of the importance of the Dedlocks, and has been unfailingly gallant towards his wife, a perfectly self-possessed woman.

Mr Tulkinghorn, the Dedlocks' solicitor, is announced. He informs them that the Jarndyce case, in which Lady Dedlock has a part, has again been in Chancery, though nothing has come out of it. Sir Leicester does not mind, an interminable Chancery suit being a 'British, constitutional kind of thing'.

However, as fresh affidavits have been brought, Mr Tulkinghorn has thought it his duty to show them to Lady Dedlock. On seeing the handwriting on one of these papers, she is startled and almost faints. She leaves the room.

NOTES AND GLOSSARY:

Rip van Winkle: a game of ninepins seemed like thunder to Washington Irving's character

baronet: hereditary title of the lowest rank

how Alexander wept: Plutarch informs us that Alexander wept when he was told of the existence of an infinite number of worlds because he had 'not yet conquered one'

as if the present baronet ... whole set: a coin is made to disappear by a conjurer and is eventually discovered inside a locked box, itself the smallest of a whole set of boxes

a Mercury in powder: footman with abundantly powdered hair. Mercury, the messenger of the gods, also guided the souls of the dead to the underworld

librarian: bookseller. Librarians could also be agents for entertainments and provide, for instance, freaks at high society parties

Wat Tyler: leader of the Peasants' Revolt in 1381. Note that young Rouncewell is also called Watt, though this might be an allusion to James Watt, Scottish pioneer of steam power

law-hand: particular type of handwriting used for legal documents. As Nemo has taken rather late to law-hand his original handwriting is not fully disguised

---

Chapter 3: A Progress (*Esther's narrative*)

In her self-deprecating way Esther Summerson describes her earliest years at Windsor, her doll, the only thing she would confide in, and her godmother, a grave, strict, awe-inspiring person who never smiled.

Esther had never known her father or mother, and had been told nothing about them. She did not know her fellow-pupils at school well, and Mrs Rachael, the only servant, was uncommunicative. On one of her birthdays, the most melancholy day of the whole year, Esther asked her godmother once more about her mama.

Her godmother's face, she noticed, quite clearly told her, that 'it would have been far better . . . that you had never been born'. She is told that her mother is her 'disgrace', that she wronged her godmother, and that Esther herself was not born 'in common sinfulness and wrath'.

Esther remembers being briefly introduced to a portly gentleman, dressed in black, who scrutinised her quite closely and who was to reappear after her godmother's death about two years later, introducing himself as Mr Kenge.

Esther is now told that Miss Barbary, her godmother, was her aunt, though she is without any knowledge at all of the Jarndyce and Jarndyce suit that Mr Kenge mentions. He tells her that two years ago he was instructed that she could move to the house of a 'highly humane, but singular man', whom he represents in Jarndyce and Jarndyce. The offer is renewed now that Esther is without any relations. Mr Jarndyce, her benefactor, will have her sent to a first-rate school. Esther, barely able to speak, gratefully accepts the offer and a week later she takes her cold and melancholic leave from her godmother's house, left to Mrs Rachael, who without any regrets kisses her goodbye.

Esther, sorrowful and depressed, journeys by coach towards Reading, comforted by a kind man who happens to be travelling in the same coach, and who gets out shortly before her own destination.

Esther spends six happy years at Greenleaf, a select boarding school for twelve young ladies, run by the twin Miss Donnys. All the girls soon become fond of Esther, who helps with the teaching. About twice a year Esther writes a letter of thanks to Mr Kenge, and she receives a prompt reply that everything 'is duly communicated to our client'. These replies are signed in another hand.

One day she receives a much abbreviated note from the firm of Kenge and Carboy, informing her that she is to act as a companion to a Ward of Court whom Mr Jarndyce is about to receive into his house. Five days later Esther leaves the school for London; this time everybody deeply regrets to see her go.

A young man, splotched with ink, takes her to Lincoln's Inn, through streets filled with a dense fog. The youth leaves her in Mr Kenge's office to 'look at herself' as she is now going to the Chancellor. Presently Mr Kenge appears and brings her to the Chancellor's comfortable quarters. Here she is introduced to Ada Clare, whose companion she is to be at Mr Jarndyce's, and to a distant cousin of Ada, Richard Carstone, a handsome, light-hearted boy.

The three of them are orphans. They are taken to the Lord Chancellor, who informs Ada and Richard that they will be wards in the home of Mr Jarndyce at Bleak House in Hertfordshire. When being asked whether Esther is related to any party in the cause, Mr Kenge whispers something to the Chancellor.

The interview is over, Mr Kenge has absented himself for some minutes, and a little old woman approaches the three young people outside on the pavement. She curtseys to them, and says that she herself was a ward once, is now mad, expects a judgment shortly, on the Day of Judgment, and that she is regularly at the court with her 'documents'. Mr Kenge appears and sends her away.

NOTES AND GLOSSARY:

pray daily ... written: see the Bible, Numbers 14:18
period: elaborate, rhetorical sentence
I saw the gravestones from the staircase window: a graveyard at Lincoln's Inn Chapel
bag wig: the back hair was held in a silk bag (bag wigs were out of fashion at that time)
like the children in the wood: In the ballad 'The Children of the Wood' brother and sister are abandoned in a forest
Bleak House: see 'Setting' on p. 10 of these notes
the sixth seal: Miss Flite equals the sixth seal of St John's vision (see the Bible, Revelations 6:12) with the Great Seal of England. The opening of the sixth seal was to bring calamities

---

Chapter 4: Telescopic Philanthropy (*Esther's narrative*)

Ada, Esther and Richard are to spend the night at the house of Mrs Jellyby, a lady wholly devoted to philanthropic projects, especially to the 'subject of Africa'. Mr Kenge is astonished that they should never have heard anything of her. Her husband, however, can be described only as 'the husband of Mrs Jellyby'. Mr Kenge takes his leave and the same ink-stained lad, Mr Guppy, who pays a compliment to the embarrassed Esther, brings them to the Jellybys' place. There they first meet with a child that has got its head caught in the railings; they then encounter other children, one of them (Peepy) painfully tumbling downstairs. Nobody seems to mind. The house is incredibly messy and dirty. Ada and Esther meet Mrs Jellyby, and Esther shows kindness towards the children. Mrs Jellyby's time is completely taken up by the Borrioboola-Gha natives, and her shy, overworked eldest daughter, Caddy, is working as her secretary. In writing about Mrs Jellyby, Dickens may have been inspired by an expedition, organised by the

African Civilisation Society and the Niger Association, which went to the Upper Niger in the 1840s.

Eventually an undercooked dinner is served under chaotic conditions. A quiet man is also present, who turns out to be Mr Jellyby. In the evening, Mr Quale appears, introducing himself as a philanthropist.

Having retired, Ada and Esther wonder about Mr Jarndyce, whom neither of them has ever met. Caddy enters their room, feeling very miserable, and wishing that 'Africa was dead'. Caddy is all too conscious of her shabby surroundings. Esther comforts her and she cries herself to sleep. At dawn, little Peepy also comes to Esther's room, trembling with cold.

NOTES AND GLOSSARY:

toucher:	bowl that touches the scoring-pin in lawn-bowling
beadle:	minor parish official, who also had some civil functions
area:	lower lying narrow court between pavement and front-door, giving access to the basement where the servants lived
pattens:	thick-soled overshoes used in bad weather or muddy places

---

Chapter 5: A Morning Adventure (*Esther's narrative*)

Early in the morning Caddy suggests they go for a walk. Esther washes Peepy, who goes to sleep again. The three girls leave the depressingly dirty house and outside meet Richard, who has been 'dancing up and down Thavies Inn to warm his feet.' Caddy walks them quickly through the streets, apparently without any precise aim. On her way she vehemently complains about her mother's activities and her mismanagement. She also bitterly resents Mr Quale's officious courtship of her.

The party reaches Lincoln's Inn. 'We are never to get out of Chancery,' Richard says. They meet the old lady again, who, still crazily talking about Chancery and 'the Sixth Seal', invites them to her lodgings.

They come to a narrow lane in the immediate neighbourhood of the Inn and to a shop over which is written KROOK, RAG AND BOTTLE WAREHOUSE. A great many inscriptions in the window make Esther think that 'everything seemed to be bought, and nothing to be sold there'. Some of these inscriptions are written in 'law-hand', like the letters she used to get from Kenge and Carboy's office. One notice, in the same hand, is asking for copying work, to be executed by 'Nemo', who lives above the shop. (Esther, so far in the story, knows nothing of Lady Dedlock or Tulkinghorn and the hand-writing incident in Chapter 2.)

They meet Krook, a 'short, cadaverous and withered' man, 'the breath issuing in visible smoke from his mouth, as if he were on fire within', who is called the 'Lord Chancellor,' and his jumbled store the 'Chancery'.

Once Krook knows that he is talking to 'the wards in Jarndyce', he tells them about the death of Tom Jarndyce, who shot himself. According to Tom Jarndyce, being involved in a chancery cause was 'like being drowned by drops'.

The three young people are led to the old lady's shabby and bare, but clean garret. Esther now understands the poor woman's pinched appearance: she is almost starving. She keeps several birds in cages. They are to be released on the day that judgement is given, but their lives are too short and they die in prison, she informs her guests.

The neighbouring bells make her gather her bags and hurry back to court. On their way downstairs she points to the other lodger's (the law writer's) door and says that according to the local children he has 'sold his soul to the devil'.

Krook, nearly illiterate, makes Esther undergo one more uncanny experience: he chalks the words 'Jarndyce – Bleak House' upon the wall, beginning with the end of each letter and shaping it backwards, for he has never learnt to write, but copies from memory.

At last they leave this weird place, with Ada prophetically musing about the enmities and disasters this wasteful case may raise. Back at the Jellybys', breakfast is eventually ready, and at one o'clock a carriage arrives to take Ada, Esther and Richard to Bleak House.

NOTES AND GLOSSARY:

pewter-pots:	beer mugs. A 'pot boy' would collect these mugs, that had been brought from a neighbouring bar
vacation:	see the note on law-courts, p. 10
Nemo:	(*Latin*) nobody
counsellors' bands:	a kind of tie worn by lawyers
Lady Jane:	the name perhaps refers to Lady Jane Grey, Queen Mary's predecessor on the throne of England (she was executed in 1554)

Chapter 6: Quite at Home (*Esther's narrative*)

They have a pleasant drive westward, passing Mr Jarndyce's waggoner who has notes delivered to them by their guardian that they should 'meet as old friends, and take the past for granted.' Ada and Richard both vaguely remember that their benefactor dislikes all signs of gratitude.

They reach Bleak House, near St Albans, at night and are given a warm welcome by John Jarndyce. Esther recognises in him the kind gentleman she met in the coach six years ago. Mr Jarndyce enquires about Mrs Jellyby, and, having been told that the Jellyby children are 'in a devil of a state', reacts by saying that 'the wind is in the east', which is his way of showing annoyance or discomfort.

They are then shown the vast rambling house, the furniture of which reflects both the generosity and the sensitivity of its owner. Esther and Ada have separate rooms, but they will share a delightful sitting-room. Before going down for dinner a maid brings Esther the housekeeping keys. Esther is surprised and almost overcome by the trust shown in her.

Mr Jarndyce has told the wards that there will be a guest, Mr Harold Skimpole, whom Esther describes as having more the appearance of 'a damaged young man, than a well-preserved elderly one'. Skimpole is still a mere child who has never known anything about money, according to Mr Jarndyce and according to himself. But the wind is again 'in the east', when Richard asks about Skimpole's large family.

Skimpole rather cheekily tells his new friends that they ought to be grateful to him, for giving them the opportunity of enjoying 'the luxury of generosity'.

While he is prattling away, Ada plays the piano and Richard lovingly watches her. Esther cannot help noticing the thoughtful, but benignant looks Mr Jarndyce gives to the pair.

Skimpole and Richard have withdrawn after tea and the maid calls Esther for help: Mr Skimpole has been 'took'!

He has, however, not been taken ill but is going to be arrested for debt by 'Coavinses' (Neckett). As Skimpole has already sponged on Jarndyce, he will now try to get the money from Richard. Both Richard and Esther will settle his debt with whatever money they have.

Mr Jarndyce, on hearing about this arrangement, feels that 'the wind's round again!' Esther soothes him, though Mr Jarndyce insists that there will be no more advances for Skimpole.

NOTES AND GLOSSARY:

Whittington: Richard ('Dick') Whittington was a poor boy, who eventually broke the bars of class and was Lord Mayor of London three times during the Hundred Years War

Barnet-an old battle-field: site of the Battle of Barnet (1471), where the Yorkists defeated the Lancastrians during the Wars of the Roses

the wind's in the east: the east wind is supposed to bring bad weather. It could also bring smells and pollution from London's East End to its West End and to St Albans

Captain Cook: Captain Cook was killed by Hawaiian natives in 1779. Engravings showing the murder were popular

ladies... in short waists: a late eighteenth-century fashion with the waistline very high

Queen Anne: Queen of England 1702–14

presses: closets for linen

Bristol-board: thick paper used for drawing and painting

Age or change should never wither it: compare Shakespeare's *Antony and Cleopatra* II, 2, 240–1

Coavinses: a sort of debtors' prison, named after its owner

the birds... cathedral: perhaps a reminiscence of a Shakespeare sonnet (LXXIII)

the best of all ways...: from a song by the Irish poet Thomas Moore (1779–1852)

St Michael's oranges: a type of orange coming from St Michael's Island in the Azores

cod's head and shoulders: a perfect fool

Chapter 7: The Ghost's Walk

The story moves to Chesney Wold in Lincolnshire. The large estate would be lifeless, were it not for the stables, kennels and poultry-yard.

This rain-sodden country house is looked after by old Mrs Rouncewell, the housekeeper, in whom Sir Leicester has absolute trust. Mrs Rouncewell's two sons both left Chesney Wold: the younger, a soldier, 'ran wild... and never came back'. The other's talents moved in the 'Wat Tyler direction'. He has become an ironmaster and is working in the north. His son Watt is visiting his grandmother. He enquires about the young maid Rosa, who left the room when he entered.

Presently she comes back to announce that two young men have arrived in a gig. The card she brings in announces Mr Guppy, who, with a friend, has come to the area from London on some legal business and would like to visit this stately country seat. As Guppy claims acquaintance with Mr Tulkinghorn the two young men are allowed to look around. Watt has eyes only for young Rosa, who acts as a guide. Mr Guppy and his friend are only moderately interested in the house, but a portrait of Lady Dedlock amazes, indeed almost dismays him. He feels he has seen it before – perhaps in a dream.

His interest is aroused again when Rosa points out the flagged terrace, 'The Ghost's Walk'. Mr Guppy wants to know whether the old family story that has given the terrace its name is in any way related to the portrait he has noticed. Mrs Rouncewell rather curtly tells him that the story is not told to visitors. The two young men now leave Chesney Wold.

The old housekeeper now tells Rosa and Watt the family anecdote. In the days of Charles I and Cromwell, Sir Morbury Dedlock's wife did not side with the royalists. She spied on Sir Morbury's friends, and was caught by her husband laming the royalists' horses. She herself was lamed in the ensuing scuffle. After this, becoming more and more crippled, she walked the terrace, day after day, and at her death vowed that she would go on walking those flagstones until the pride of the house was humbled.

Even now the sound, according to Mrs Rouncewell, can be heard. It is impossible to muffle, though it can be heard only when disaster or disgrace is near.

NOTES AND GLOSSARY:

solitude . . . brooding upon Chesney Wold:	see the address to the Spirit in *Paradise Lost* I, 20–1 by John Milton (1608–74)
stomacher:	woman's bodice, usually ornamented with pearls or embroidery, covering chest and stomach. An old-fashioned piece of clothing in Dickens's time
stillroom:	pantry or store-room for preserves, and so on
dreadnought:	a thick coat or cloak
out:	an outing
the blessed martyr:	Charles I, executed in 1649

Chapter 8: Covering a Multitude of Sins (*Esther's narrative*)

It is Esther's first day of housekeeping. She does the rounds of the house and the garden. Harold Skimpole, at breakfast, chatters about bees: he thinks that a drone has a most pleasant life.

Esther is called to the 'Growlery', a small room adjacent to Mr Jarndyce's bedroom, to which he retires when 'the wind is easterly.' Her guardian introduces Esther to the 'Chancery business'. The case is about a will and the administration of the trusts. Generations of lawyers, however, have managed to reduce the legatees to poverty and misery. Tom Jarndyce, her guardian's great-uncle, left the house, originally called the Peaks, a 'bleak' house. He ruined himself, poring over masses of 'wicked' Chancery papers. Part of the Jarndyce property is in London, 'The property of Costs'; it is a whole street of houses, now dilapidated.

Esther however will now be the 'good little woman . . . to sweep the cobwebs out of the sky.' She is called a whole list of other names, all relevant to her talents as a housekeeper.

Mr Jarndyce asks Esther's advice on which profession to choose for Richard, although he anticipates all the difficulties Richard may meet with at court, as he is a ward of Chancery, until his career is approved of. On being asked whether she would like to have any information on her own background, Esther gracefully declines.

Esther and Ada, who handle part of Mr Jarndyce's correspondence, are amazed to find out how many people ask their benefactor for money. Among them Mrs Pardiggle stands out for her 'rapacious benevolence'. She calls one day with her five children, who are 'ferocious with discontent', as their mother forces them to donate whatever piteous amount of pocket-money they have to foreign or obscure charities.

She now forces Ada and Esther to accompany her on one of her visiting rounds. Although Esther enjoys being confided in by children, she is embarrassed by the resentment the young Pardiggles show against their mother. They visit a poor brickmaker's family, living in a wet, wretched hovel. The husband, drunk and stretched out on the floor, describes the plight of his family with shocking realism. Mrs Pardiggle reads from a good book; she had left another such book with the brickmaker, but, as Mr Jarndyce later observed, it may be doubted 'if Robinson Crusoe could have read it, though he had had no other on his desolate island'.

When the Pardiggles have left, Ada and Esther approach the young mother, Jenny, who has been ill-used and is bent over a dying baby. As Ada touches the child, it dies. Esther covers its face with her handkerchief. The two girls come back to the house at night to bring some little comforts. Esther cannot know how important the handkerchief, which she has not reclaimed, will be for someone else later.

NOTES AND GLOSSARY:

rick-yard:	farmyard where hay was dried in stacks
brimstone:	bees were smoked out with brimstone in order to gather their honey
Manchester:	a centre of the cotton industry
off to dusty death:	see Macbeth's last monologue in Shakespeare's *Macbeth* (V.5.23)
history of the Apple Pie:	a nursery-rhyme beginning with the words 'A was an Apple Pie'
Old Woman (and Esther's nicknames):	the 'Old Woman' from a popular nursery rhyme brushed cobwebs out of the sky. Mrs or Mother Shipton was the name of a witch; Dame Durden was the main character of a popular nineteenth-century street song. Cobweb is also the name of a helpful fairy in Shakespeare's *A Midsummer Night's Dream*
Wiglomeration:	a word coined by Mr Jarndyce, synonymous with inefficiency. It might be made up of the words 'conglomeration' and 'wig' (see Chapter 1, a 'sallow prisoner ... who has fallen into a state of con- glomeration of accounts')

satellites:	the many lawyers who assist Mr Tangle (see Chapter 1)
Mrs Pardiggle, the	'Sisterhood of Medieval Marys': this lady and the 'sisterhood' recall the High Church revival at Oxford in the 1840s (Puseyism)
F.R.S.:	Fellow of the Royal Society, a highly respected philosophical society
'boned':	(*slang*) stolen
poll-pry:	behave inquisitively like Paul Pry (the title character of an early nineteenth-century comedy)

Chapter 9: Signs and Tokens (*Esther's narrative*)

Winter passes swiftly at Bleak House. Mr Jarndyce has written to a relation of the family, Sir Leicester Dedlock, in order to get his help as the sea is a likely career for Richard. But Sir Leicester politely answers that he cannot help; he also mentions the fact that Lady Dedlock is remotely related to the young man.

Esther worries about Richard, who mistakes his carelessness in financial things for prudence.

One morning Lawrence Boythorn, an old school-friend of John Jarndyce, now a neighbour of Sir Leicester in Lincolnshire, is announced.

He arrives rather late, a boisterous, stalwart man, accompanied by a tame canary. At dinner he tells his hosts that there is a permanent legal quarrel between him and Sir Leicester about some right of way. Esther is touched by Boythorn's hidden sensitivity and asks her guardian whether his friend never wanted to marry. Yes, there was a woman in Boythorn's life, but 'she died to him'.

Boythorn is waiting for some message from Kenge and Carboy, and the following morning Mr Guppy appears. His interview with Boythorn leaves Mr Guppy, now a dandyish young man, somewhat ruffled. Left alone with Esther Guppy proposes to her, going as far as to hint that he might 'advance her interests'. Esther refuses him.

NOTES AND GLOSSARY:

to get broke:	to be dismissed
Sir Lucifer:	the rebel archangel, Satan, whose pride or 'sense of injur'd merit' made him be expelled from Heaven (see the Bible, Revelation)
fire-engine:	portable water-pump
bear's grease:	fragrant pomade for the hair

Chapter 10: The Law-writer

Mr Snagsby, a law-stationer, keeps his shop near Chancery Lane. He has married the niece of his deceased partner Mr Peffer, a woman with a sharp nose 'like a sharp autumn evening', a regular shrew, who is venting all her grievances on Guster (Augusta), a poor servant-girl from the workhouse, who '"has fits" – which the parish cannot account for'.

Tulkinghorn comes to Snagsby's shop; he shows the stationer an affidavit and wants to know who copied it. Snagsby looks up the name of the copyist in his book. It was Nemo, who lives opposite the lane in a rag-and-bottle shop. He will take Mr Tulkinghorn to Nemo's lodgings. Meanwhile suspicious Mrs Snagsby looks after the shop; she also refers to the entries of her husband's book, which has been left open.

Having been shown the place Tulkinghorn heads for Lincoln's Inn, but as soon as Snagsby has gone, he goes back to Krook's shop. Krook directs him up to the second floor. The lodger lies stretched out on his bed, in an unbelievably dirty room. Tulkinghorn smells the odour of opium. Nemo does not stir.

NOTES AND GLOSSARY:

pounce:	fine pumice-stone powder, used to soak up spilled ink
wafers:	paper-made seals
ferret:	silk tape
bodkin:	pointed instrument for piercing holes
he was out of his time:	he was no longer an apprentice
Tooting:	orphanage in which children were notoriously ill-treated; 'an amiable benefactor of his species' refers to its owner, Drouet
Allegory, in Roman helmet:	Mr Tulkinghorn lives in a former 'house of state'; late eighteenth-century houses often had neo-classical paintings on walls and ceilings
Folio:	here refers to the number of words to be copied
Banshee:	supernatural being in Gaelic folklore whose wailing warns a family of an approaching death
winding-sheets:	here, the solidified drippings of a candle

Chapter 11: Our Dear Brother

Krook comes with a candle and enters the room together with Tulkinghorn. The man on the bed is dead. Tulkinghorn calls for Miss Flite to send for a doctor. In the meantime, Krook has crept to Nemo's portmanteau and back again.

A Scottish doctor arrives and pronounces Nemo dead. As there is a young man present, also of the medical profession, who used to provide Nemo with opium, the doctor leaves again. The young man says that there was something about the deceased man that denoted a fall in life. Nobody however has known him well. Only Krook insists on the fact that he owes him six weeks' rent.

Mr Tulkinghorn having stood for some while near the portmanteau, says that he wanted to offer Nemo some work on Snagsby's recommendation. Miss Flite leaves to fetch the stationer.

Mr Snagsby only remembers the man as a competent and zealous copyist, of whom his wife was rather fond. She used to call him 'Nimrod'. As there will be an inquest, Tulkinghorn has the room searched for any revealing papers; but nothing is found.

Mr Mooney, the beadle at the inquest, calls for witnesses. Mrs Piper, a cabinet-maker's wife from the neighbourhood, gives an artless report on Nemo, with no useful facts at all, except that Nemo would often speak to a boy who sweeps the streets. That boy is sent for, but whatever poor, illiterate Jo has to say is disregarded by the coroner. There is a verdict of 'accidental death'.

The court is discharged and at a nearby pub, the Sol's Arms, Little Swills, the singer, now improvises his own version of the inquest.

The following day Nemo is buried at a very shabby burial-ground. He is sown in corruption, 'to be raised in corruption'.

When night comes, Jo slouches to the rusty iron gate of the burial-ground and sweeps the archway, because Nemo 'wos wery good to me.'

NOTES AND GLOSSARY:

As dead as Phairy: as dead as Pharoah
... until Government shall abolish him (the beadle): The beadles' duties were gradually taken over by the newly established Metropolitan Police
skittles: a game similar to ninepins
bagatelle-board: a sort of billiard table
half-baptising: a sick or very weak child could be baptised privately without the full ceremony
'a rummy start': an odd incident
Guster murders sleep: compare Shakespeare's *Macbeth*, II.2.35
Tooting and her patron saint: see note to Chapter 10
Caffre: South African native, here synonymous with infidel
come night, come darkness: compare *Macbeth*, III.2.46–7

Chapter 12: On the Watch

Lady Dedlock and Sir Leicester are on their way home from Paris to Lincolnshire. It has stopped raining in Lincolnshire and Mrs

Rouncewell is preparing the house, as there will also be a small party of people from 'the world of position'.

In the coach between Paris and the coast Sir Leicester is perusing his correspondence. Lady Dedlock notices a letter in Tulkinghorn's handwriting. Her husband informs her that Tulkinghorn has seen the copyist of that affidavit 'the hand of which' stimulated her curiosity so much. Lady Dedlock makes the coach stop at once. She must have a short walk, but soon feels better and is her usual haughty self again.

They have a rough crossing, spend a night in London, and proceed to Chesney Wold. Mrs Rouncewell is there to greet them and Lady Dedlock is immediately struck by the beauty of the new young maid, Rosa. Aloof as she usually is, she cannot but pay her a touching compliment.

That evening Rosa and Mrs Rouncewell praise Lady Dedlock, whom the housekeeper regrets has no daughter herself. Young Watt, her grandson, is also present, mainly because of Rosa. He, however, resents Lady Dedlock's pride.

Hortense, Lady Dedlock's French maid, also notices her mistress's reception of Rosa. She (rightly) anticipates that Rosa will altogether win her ladyship's favour.

Chesney Wold is now crowded with dandies, snobs and ineffectual politicians. The house is quite full; but one room has been kept for Mr Tulkinghorn. Day after day Lady Dedlock casually inquires whether or not he has arrived. Hortense notices a brooding expression on her face.

At last Mr Tulkinghorn comes. He has been delayed, as he explains to Sir Leicester and Lady Dedlock, by the several suits between Sir Leicester and Boythorn.

Lady Dedlock finds an opportunity to ask casually about the letter-writer. Mr Tulkinghorn gives her all the details: he was found dead, there were no papers. Sir Leicester gallantly begs him not to expatiate on such a shocking story in Lady Dedlock's presence. She remains impassive; she will not broach the subject again, neither will Mr Tulkinghorn. But each of them hides 'what each would give to know how much the other knows'.

NOTES AND GLOSSARY:

bend-sinister:	heraldic term for a narrow stripe from the top left-hand corner to the bottom right-hand corner of a coat of arms (*sinister* (Latin) = left). Such a stripe betrayed illegitimacy
Centaurs:	mythological creatures, half man, half horse. Here, mounted horses
headless queen:	Queen Marie-Antoinette, guillotined in 1793
Giant Despair:	Allegorical figure from John Bunyan's *The Pilgrim's Progress* (1678)

Ariel:	Puck in Shakespeare's *A Midsummer Night's Dream* (II.1.175) 'put a girdle round the earth'. Dickens confused him with Ariel in *The Tempest*
Jacob's dream:	see the Bible, Genesis 28:12
mighty hunter:	Nimrod (see the Bible, Genesis 10:8–9); the following lines compare people being introduced to the Monarch with a fox leaving his hiding-place (or cover)
towel neckcloth:	a cloth rolled round the neck
false calves:	padded stockings
buckskins:	tight-fitting breeches made of soft leather
... the self-reproach of having once consumed a pea:	an anecdote ascribed to a well-known dandy, Beau Brummell (1778–1840)
necromancer:	sorcerer
some leads:	lead-covered roof

Chapter 13: Esther's Narrative

Richard's fickle character worries Mr Jarndyce and Esther. He has not yet settled on a profession. Mr Jarndyce partly blames the influence of Chancery for Richard's indecisive behaviour. Esther is rather sceptical about the young man's public-school education. Richard seems to have been mainly taught the art of versification.

On a mere suggestion from Mr Jarndyce, however, Richard says he wants to become a surgeon. Mr Kenge's advice is sought. He suggests that Richard should stay with a suitable practitioner. As his cousin is in the medical profession Richard might as well be placed with him.

At the end of Mr Boythorn's visit, they all move to London for a few weeks. Esther enjoys the sights of the city, but she is embarrassed by Mr Guppy again, while at a theatre. Sitting in front of the box with her friends Esther notices the woeful face of the young man, perpetually gazing up at her. In fact Guppy is present at any theatre they go to, always in the same romantic attitude.

Richard is placed with Kenge's cousin Mr Bayham Badger, a practitioner in Chelsea who will superintend his medical studies. The whole party is invited to dine at the Badgers' house one night and they are surprised that Mr Badger exceedingly admires his wife for having had three husbands. After dinner Mrs Badger describes her former husbands.

Esther cannot help noticing the growing attachment between Ada and Richard. Back home again, Ada confides in Esther that she and Richard are in love. Esther promises that she will talk to John Jarndyce. Their guardian insists on the seriousness and beauty of marriage; he also urges

Richard to work steadily. When the young pair has left, Mr Jarndyce can barely conceal his own love for Esther.

Very abruptly we are told that Esther has noticed someone else at the Badgers' dinner-party – a young surgeon of a dark complexion. Esther thinks he is very agreeable.

NOTES AND GLOSSARY:

M.R.C.S.: Member of the Royal College of Surgeons
dreadful spikes: spikes attached to the rear axle of a carriage
all a taunto: with all sails hoisted
the heathen waggoner: a waggoner who prayed the gods for help because his waggon was stuck in the mud (compare Aesop's Fables)

Chapter 14: Deportment (*Esther's narrative*)

Richard leaves for Mr Badger's place. Though apparently eager to study medicine, he nevertheless very much relies on the Chancery suit, the court being, according to him, his and Ada's guardian. Ada would rather forget all about it.

As they are in London, Ada and Esther want to call on Mrs Jellyby; but with her many duties she is never at home. One morning, however, Caddy comes to see them. She has brought her little brother Peepy with her. The boy's clothes are so ridiculously shabby that Mr Jarndyce has to withdraw into his temporary London Growlery at once. Peepy being out of earshot, Caddy, who has become much prettier, reports on the situation of her family: Mr Jellyby is threatened by bankruptcy, Mrs Jellyby doesn't care about anything, and everybody feels more wretched than ever before.

Caddy lets her two friends into a secret: she is going to leave her chaotic family; she is engaged. Since meeting Ada and Esther, she has felt ill at ease at home; she started improving herself and took dancing lessons; and she is now engaged to Mr Prince Turveydrop, the son of the owner of the Dancing Academy. Caddy frequently meets Prince at Miss Flite's.

Esther accompanies Caddy to the Dancing Academy. Prince is a very hard-working young man, but everything is false about old Mr Turveydrop; in fact Esther believes she sees 'creases come into the whites of his eyes', when he bows to her. She immediately dislikes him.

After the class, Esther and Caddy walk to Lincoln's Inn to Miss Flite's, where they also find John Jarndyce and Ada. On her way upstairs, Esther is chilled by the desolate atmosphere of Nemo's empty room. Caddy is able to do some small jobs for Miss Flite, who is introducing her to the household chores. Miss Flite has been unwell ever since Nemo's death, and a young medical gentleman, Mr Woodcourt, is there to look after her.

Mr Woodcourt asks the visitors if they have heard of Miss Flite's good fortune. The old lady presently explains that she is given seven shillings by Mr Kenge or Mr Guppy every Saturday, one for each day of the week. She suspects that the Lord Chancellor, who smiled at her the other day, provides her with the money through Kenge's office. Esther suspects the source to be Mr Jarndyce.

Krook, followed by his nightmarish cat, intrudes upon the party and reels off the names of Miss Flite's twenty-five birds. They have allegorical names such as Hope, Ruin, Folly, and are imprisoned, as Krook insists, by his noble and learned brother, the Lord Chancellor.

As he is known as the local Lord Chancellor, he insists that Mr Jarndyce, for whom the wind is very much in the east now, should see his own Court of Chancery.

Having left distrustful Krook and his depressing 'Chancery' they all have a merry evening at Mr Jarndyce's London house.

Esther tells us that Mr Woodcourt is the same young surgeon she met at Mr Badger's. We guess that, instead of talking about Richard, Ada wants to tease Esther into talking about Mr Woodcourt.

NOTES AND GLOSSARY:

cane forms: benches

his illustrious model on a sofa: a reference to a portrait of George IV

Gammon and Spinach: in this context, 'Deceit' and 'Falsehood'

Chapter 15: Bell Yard

While in London, Mr Jarndyce is beleaguered by philanthropists, among them Mr Quale. Skimpole gives a cheeky report of his incurring debts. Quite casually he mentions the death of Coavinses, the debt-collector ('arrested by the great Bailiff'). Coavinses has left three orphans. Mr Jarndyce and his party immediately set out to help, directed by Skimpole. They find the children at kind-hearted Mrs Blinder's in Bell Yard. Another of Mrs Blinder's lodgers is Gridley, a sallow man, who has been a victim of the court of Equity for more than twenty-five years (he is the 'man from Shropshire' mentioned in Chapter 1). Neckett's (Coavinses') children have been locked up in their poor room by their elder sister Charley. The visitors find a six-year-old boy who is nursing a heavy baby of eighteen months. Although Gridley is a bitter and resentful man, he is nevertheless kind to these children, whom he has befriended. He takes the two younger ones with him to his room, when their sister is off to work again. Skimpole, in his usual frivolous way, says that he was a benefactor of Coavinses, because without him

Coavinses could not have brought up his children. Surprisingly enough, he seems to cheer up Mr Jarndyce.

NOTES AND GLOSSARY:
widow's mite: see the Bible, Mark 12:42
he proposes to frank me down and back again: he proposes to pay my expenses
unharmonious blacksmith: an allusion to an air by G. F. Handel, commonly called 'The Harmonious Blacksmith'

Chapter 16: Tom-all-Alone's

Lady Dedlock has become very restless; she has gone to London, while her husband stays at Chesney Wold in the grips of the gout.

Jo, the crossing-sweeper, has come out of his horrible slum-dwellings, called Tom-all-Alone's, and is doing his job. Jo, according to the author, 'lives – that is to say, he has not died.' The estate is in Chancery; the suit of Jarndyce and Jarndyce has ruined these houses.

A veiled lady passes Mr Tulkinghorn's chambers. He is thinking of having Gridley arrested, because he finds him 'alarming'. The veiled lady beckons to Jo; she has read about him in the paper, and she asks him to show her the places that the dead copyist used to frequent. Thus she passes Snagsby's and Krook's shops and is finally brought to that dismal graveyard where Nemo is buried.

That night Lady Dedlock attends a grand dinner and several balls. Sir Leicester can distinctly hear the ghost's steps on the terrace.

NOTES AND GLOSSARY:
'the memory of man goeth not to the contrary': from time immemorial
the tee-totum: a spinning-top, here meaning London
fly: artful
Fen larks: no tricks
Stow hooking it: don't run away
half a bull: half a crown, twelve and a half new pence

Chapter 17: Esther's Narrative

Esther regrets that Richard's education did not develop any habit of concentration; indeed there is something of a gamester about him. Mrs Bayham Badger visits the two girls and tells them that Richard 'has not chosen his profession advisedly'; she compares him to Allan Woodcourt, a much more persevering young man.

Next evening Richard comes. He says that the professional course he is taking now will 'do as well as anything else'. Esther is seriously worried by his shallowness and flippancy, and even Ada, infatuated as she is, is almost afraid when Richard says that he wants to start studying law now.

The girls suggest that Richard seek the advice of Mr Jarndyce, who is still as benevolent as ever, but is also more thoughtful.

That night Esther, unable to sleep, wants to finish some needlework and goes to the temporary Growlery to get some silk. She is surprised at finding her guardian there, looking quite weary. John Jarndyce has decided to tell Esther what he knows about her earlier years.

Nine years before he had received a letter from an unknown woman (Miss Barbary) using cruel and heartless language about a young girl in her custody, but also asking him to finish that young girl's education in the event of the writer's early death. Mr Jarndyce is unable to elucidate the 'disgrace' of Esther's birth. Esther thanks her guardian for his fatherly behaviour, but John Jarndyce seems to be troubled by her grateful words.

Allan Woodcourt, who is leaving for China and India as a ship's surgeon, pays a farewell visit. He is accompanied by his snobbish mother, who, by insisting too much on Allan's pedigree and on the importance of a suitable alliance for him, adds much to Esther's sorrow at Allan's departure.

That same day Caddy comes to see Esther. She finds her feverishly working, trying to overcome her sadness – though she does not admit this. Caddy has brought a nosegay, left at Miss Flite's for Esther by 'Somebody' who had to take a ship.

NOTES AND GLOSSARY:

junk:	salt meat used on sea voyages
earings:	line used to fasten a corner of a sail to the yard
pipe-claying:	to clean clothes or to whiten leather with white clay, here 'settling their bills'
Blackstone:	Sir William Blackstone (1723–80) was the author of *Commentaries of the Laws of England* (1765–9)
Minerva:	Roman goddess of wisdom and learning

Chapter 18: Lady Dedlock (*Esther's narrative*)

Richard, after much hesitation, is now on an experimental course at Kenge and Carboy's. Mr Jarndyce, though evidently displeased, helps him to find lodgings. Richard will now try to disentangle the secrets of the fatal suit of Jarndyce and Jarndyce.

The girls, accompanied by their guardian and Skimpole, travel north to Lincolnshire to visit Mr Boythorn, who is waiting for them with an open carriage at a small market-town. Their host does not take them to his house on a direct road, as this would mean crossing 'Sir Arrogant

Numskull's' [Sir Leicester's] land. Esther, on being shown Chesney Wold from a distance, is impressed by a feeling of repose. In the village they meet young Rouncewell, who has come to see Rosa again.

Boythorn has a pleasant old house in a beautiful flower-garden, though one side of his estate is grimly guarded against a possible Dedlock aggression.

While attending church next day, Esther sees young Rouncewell again, his eyes riveted on Rosa. Lady Dedlock's French maid is present as well. Sir Leicester and Lady Dedlock arrive at the beginning of the service. Esther is struck by the sight of her ladyship; memories of her early years at her godmother's are stirred. Lady Dedlock's face is 'in a confused way, like a broken glass' to Esther. She is, however, unable to explain the reason for her tension, which has not escaped the watchful French maid.

Skimpole declares himself impressed by Sir Leicester, because the baronet is able to offer agreeable things. He readily agrees that he has no principles, thereby shocking and irritating Boythorn. Esther is astonished that Skimpole never mentions his family.

About a week later, Esther, Ada and Mr Jarndyce are surprised by a storm, while walking through the Dedlock woods. They find shelter in an old, dark lodge. Ada mistakes a voice behind her for Esther's; it is in fact Lady Dedlock who has spoken; she has taken shelter in the same lodge shortly before their arrival. She politely but not indifferently talks to Mr Jarndyce and also inquires about Richard. Mr Jarndyce knew Lady Dedlock and her sister many years ago.

A pony carriage with Hortense and Rosa comes to fetch Lady Dedlock. She takes her leave of Ada and Mr Jarndyce, ignoring Esther. She then drives back with Rosa, snubbing Hortense. The French maid steps out of her shoes and ostentatiously walks home barefooted through the wettest grass. The keeper of the lodge suggests that she is doing this to cool her blood; his wife, however, thinks that Hortense fancies she walks through blood.

NOTES AND GLOSSARY:

Fortunatus's purse: purse with an inexhaustible fund
phaeton: light carriage
Ajax: Ajax on his way home from the Trojan war was struck by lightning
list: cloth
blunderbuss: old-fashioned short gun with a broad muzzle
Milton's cloud: see *Comus* (lines 223–4)

Chapter 19: Moving On

The long vacation has started in Chancery Lane. The members of the bar of England have their holiday abroad and London is idle and sleepy during a very hot summer. Even Krook is sitting outside pursuing his studies, his cat at his side.

The Snagsbys have visitors – Mr and Mrs Chadband. Mr Chadband is a self-appointed minister of a congregation that has no precise denomination, but Mrs Snagsby dotes on him. While Mr Chadband develops his ideas and helps himself generously at table, Guster, whose endeavours at correct behaviour have been disastrous, tells her master that he is wanted in the shop.

Mr Snagsby finds a police constable holding by the arm a ragged boy, Jo, who refuses 'to move on'. Snagsby concedes that he knows Jo, but, as his wife has turned up, he will not mention the money he gave the poor boy at the inquest on Nemo's death.

Mr Guppy arrives. He told the constable that the boy was known to Mr Snagsby. Jo must explain to the suspicious constable where he got the two half-crowns that were found in his pockets. They are all that is left of a sovereign given to him by a lady, who was much interested in Nemo's fate. Guppy's interest is roused and he questions Jo. Guppy and the crossing-sweeper are invited upstairs by Mr Snagsby. Guppy finds out that Mrs Chadband was, years ago, placed in charge of a little girl called Esther Summerson, who was 'put out in life' by Kenge and Carboy.

Mr Chadband's sermons only elicit a yawn from Jo. The Chadbands leave and Snagsby slips some left-over food to Jo, which he eats in a nook of Blackfriars Bridge, before being told to move on.

NOTES AND GLOSSARY:

laid up in ordinary: a ship is 'laid up' when out of commission

the Flying Dutchman: a legendary ship doomed to drift about for ever

javelin-men, white wands: officers who carried white staves when attending a judge on ceremonial occasions

as merry as a grig: quite happy

Palladium: the bar of England is compared to the statue (Palladium) of Pallas Athena. The safety of Troy was supposed to depend on that statue

Bark A 1: first-class boat

train oil: oil from a marine animal ('train' derives from the Dutch word for oil)

One thousing seven hunderd and eighty-two: Guster refers in her own way to a number on the driver's badge

gonoph: pickpocket

be-all and end-all: compare Shakespeare's *Macbeth* (I.7.5)
drains: (*slang*) drinks

Chapter 20: A New Lodger

Guppy is chafing in Kenge and Carboy's offices, envious of Richard Carstone, whom he calls a 'swell'. Guppy and young Smallweed, an office-boy, have a visit from Jobling, a friend and confidant of theirs, who is now out of work and desperately short of money.

Smallweed takes them to a vulgar eating-house and we come to know that it was Jobling who accompanied Mr Guppy to Chesney Wold (see Chapter 7). Guppy pays for a copious meal and manages to talk Jobling into accepting some sort of spying job for him at Krook's. Jobling could take Nemo's room, do some copying work for Snagsby under an assumed name, and could try, at the same time, to find out what Krook is 'up to'.

They repair to Krook's shop and find the old man fast asleep, an empty gin bottle beside him. They wake him with some difficulty, and, having fetched some more gin from the Sol's Arms, Guppy introduces Jobling as Mr Weevle. 'Weevle' will now take over Nemo's room, which has been cleaned and whitewashed. The following day Weevle starts furnishing the room, decorating it with pictures of fashionable people, and at once becomes popular with the ladies of the neighbourhood.

NOTES AND GLOSSARY:
swell:	smart, fashionable person
Slap-Bang:	modest eating-house with poor service
Doe and Roe:	fictitious names for plaintiff and defendant
half-and-half:	mixture of two different kinds of ale
grass:	'sparrow-grass', asparagus
Ill fo manger:	*Il faut manger* (*French*), one must eat (in order to survive)
on the tapis:	being considered

Chapter 21: The Smallweed Family

The Smallweeds live at Mount Pleasant, although the neighbourhood has nothing pleasant about it. Bart Smallweed (Guppy's friend) lives here with his twin sister Judy and his grandparents. Grandfather Smallweed, his legs paralysed, spends a life totally given to avarice, in a black horse-hair armchair, faced by his imbecile wife, who has a cushion thrown at her whenever she opens her mouth. Bart comes home and listens to his dead father being praised by miserly old Smallweed. The Smallweeds' maid, Charley (Coavinses' daughter; see Chapter 15), is given the poor remains of their tea. Her shabby meal is interrupted when she has to announce 'Mr George', a former trooper, whose evident generosity sharply contrasts with the bleak and stingy atmosphere of the Smallweed household. Mr George, we find out, has been an unruly son in his youth; he was also a friend of a Captain Hawdon, who died a little time ago. Both George and Hawdon have borrowed money from Old Smallweed and George has come to pay his bi-monthly interest. If ever George were late in paying, we are darkly aware, it would mean the end of his 'bisiness'.

George now leaves, and, after a visit to a theatre, turns to his business: a shooting gallery. George's helper, Phil Squod, takes out their bedding, and both go to sleep, at opposite ends of the room. Phil Squod, a foundling, was discovered in the gutter, by a watchman.

NOTES AND GLOSSARY:

porter's chair:	chair beneath a hood-like structure to protect the person sitting in it from draughts
. . . over the water to Charley:	a quotation from a song honouring Charles Stuart (Bonnie Prince Charlie, 1720–88)
cherubim:	an order of angels. Dickens here alludes to Sir Joshua Reynolds's (1723–92) *Study of Heads*
trivet:	three-legged stand or small table
black draught:	laxative
Druidical ruin:	the crusts of bread are reminiscent of an old monument, such as Stonehenge
Dead March in Saul:	from Handel's oratorio *Saul* (1738)
I'll lime you:	I'll catch you with lime (like a bird)
swipes:	watery beer

Chapter 22: Mr Bucket

Mr Tulkinghorn, not minding the dust that has settled in his office, sits and sips his fine port. Mr Snagsby, who has managed to get away from his inquisitive wife, is present as well, relating Jo's statement about the unknown, veiled lady he took to Nemo's lodgings and grave. Mr Tulkinghorn, though quite interested, remains perfectly calm. His guest is startled by the presence of a third person whom he has overlooked in the darkness of the room. This is Mr Bucket, a detective officer. Snagsby goes to help him to find Jo, after he has been told that Jo won't be harmed. Both proceed to Tom-all-Alone's, and move through the worst slums imaginable. They eventually come upon 'Toughy's' lair. Toughy is out, fetching some medicine for a sick woman, Liz (see Chapter 8). She has come from St Albans, tramping together with her friend Jenny and their husbands, both brickmakers.

When Toughy turns up, he is immediately recognised as Jo by Snagsby. He tells his story again and is led off to Tulkinghorn's rooms.

At Tulkinghorn's Jo is shown a veiled female figure. He recognises the garments, but the hand, the voice, are different. Bucket simulates dissatisfaction; Jo is paid and dismissed. Mr Tulkinghorn enters the room, the lady raises her veil. She is Hortense, Lady Dedlock's previous maid. Hortense asks Tulkinghorn to find her some new employment. Bucket is satisfied: The lady Jo saw was wearing Hortense's clothes. Snagsby returns to his 'little woman'.

NOTES AND GLOSSARY:

smallclothes:	close-fitting knee-breeches (old-fashioned in Dickens's day)
lay:	place of work
bull's-eye:	here, lantern with a lens
palanquin:	litter or sedan-chair

Chapter 23: Esther's Narrative

After a pleasant six-week stay at Mr Boythorn's, Esther returns to Bleak House. She did not see Lady Dedlock any more, except at church, but her face kept on troubling her, always recalling moments of her earliest childhood. Before Esther leaves, Hortense visits her. She has left Lady Dedlock's service and would like to become Esther's maid. Esther does not accept her. Hortense, before leaving, gives an explanation of her strange behaviour after the storm (see Chapter 18). She walked home without her shoes because she had taken an oath, and wanted to 'stamp it on her mind.'

Richard visits Ada regularly, but Esther cannot help feeling disturbed by his getting more and more entangled with Chancery. Although pitying Miss Flite, whom he now sees daily, Richard does not notice the parallels between his situation and Miss Flite's.

Esther is worried and arranges to meet Richard in private one day while going to see Caddy Jellyby. Richard is over-optimistic about the outcome of the case, though he confesses that he is unable to settle down with any profession. Furthermore, he has got into debt and has now developed a liking for the army, a career he may drop when he is in possession of the money he expects. According to Esther, whatever qualities Richard possesses are touched by a fatal blight.

Caddy and Esther go for a short walk while Prince is giving a lesson in the neighbourhood. Esther has urged Caddy to tell her parents about her engagement and she now agrees to be present when Caddy and Prince break the news to old Mr Turveydrop and to Mr and Mrs Jellyby.

At first Mr Turveydrop groans and sobs, but when he is assured that he will remain the master of the house and will not lack in any comfort he wishes the young couple 'a long life to share with him'.

Caddy and Esther then proceed to Thavies Inn where the Jellybys live. Things have much deteriorated in the meantime: Mr Jellyby is facing bankruptcy, while his wife is still busy with her African correspondence. Her reaction, when being told about the engagement, is cold. She regrets that Caddy has not accepted Mr Quale (Chapter 4), one of the 'first philanthropists of our time'. All in all, Mrs Jellyby is completely indifferent to her daughter's happiness and returns to her correspondence. Though Caddy feels low, Esther, while riding home, is confident that her marriage will be a success.

Back at Bleak House, Esther is surprised to meet Charley (Coavinses' eldest daughter, servant to the Smallweeds), whom Mr Jarndyce has engaged to be her maid. Her brother Tom is at school, while Mrs Blinder (see Chapter 15) looks after little Emma. They may see each other once a month.

NOTES AND GLOSSARY:

key: here, a special key to allow access to the garden in the centre of Soho Square, London

second gentleman in Europe: the Prince Regent was known as the 'first gentleman in Europe'

sear and yellow leaf: compare Shakespeare's *Macbeth*, V.3.23

Chapter 24: An Appeal Case (*Esther's narrative*)

After long negotiations with the Lord Chancellor, who describes him as a 'capricious infant', Richard is at last with the Horse Guards as an applicant for an Ensign's commission.

Richard and John Jarndyce become estranged, when Mr Jarndyce states in very clear terms to Richard that the army can only be the very last professional choice, that he has exhausted whatever resources he had, and that he should not rely on the outcome of the Chancery suit, 'the family curse'. Mr Jarndyce even advises Ada and Richard to give up any ties but those of relationship.

Esther and her guardian accompany Richard to London. Mr George (see Chapter 21) comes to their lodging to give Richard fencing lessons; even George must acknowledge that Richard lacks perseverance. He has seen Esther before, he thinks, but Esther denies this. Questioned about his shooting gallery, Mr George tells Mr Jarndyce that all sorts of people can be found there: he had Frenchwomen who were good at pistol shooting, but also Mr Gridley, who must now hide from the police.

Before Richard leaves for Ireland, Esther humours him and accompanies him to the Court of Chancery, as the case is up again.

Esther is astonished that no one seems to be concerned or in a hurry to hasten the procedures.

Guppy is there, arranging papers for Mr Kenge, and he introduces Mrs Chadband to Esther, who recognises her as Mrs Rachael from her godmother's house.

As Richard and Esther are leaving, they meet Mr George, who is looking for Miss Flite. He must take her to his shooting gallery, where the dying Gridley has taken refuge.

They arrive at the shooting gallery together with a physician. Once inside, the 'physician' turns out to be Mr Bucket, the detective, who has found out about Gridley and wants to arrest him. Gridley takes Miss Flite's hand: between the two of them there has been 'a tie of many suffering years . . . the only tie that Chancery has not broken'. Bucket is compassionate and tries to rouse Gridley, but it is too late. The 'man from Shropshire' dies.

NOTES AND GLOSSARY:

Ensign:	commissioned officer in the navy or coast guard
dabs:	skilful persons, experts
spencer:	short, waist-length jacket
peace-warrant:	warrant of arrest issued by a Justice of the Peace
William Tell:	legendary Swiss hero, famous as a marksman with his crossbow

Chapter 25: Mrs Snagsby Sees It All

Mr Snagsby has become depressed since his visit to Tom-all-Alone's with Bucket; he is conscious of being involved in some secret, without being able to understand things. His wife, however, has become more jealous and irritable than ever before. Mr Chadband has forced Jo to come once more to Mr Snagsby's in order to be converted in the name of 'Terewth' (truth). Seeing her husband and Jo, Mrs Snagsby suspects that Mr Snagsby is the boy's father. She has a fit of jealousy and is brought away. Jo escapes, but Guster offers him a meal. Mr Snagsby gives Jo another half-crown and tells him not to breathe a word about what he saw at Tulkinghorn's.

NOTES AND GLOSSARY:

lay-figure:	wooden dummy used by artists to show the disposition of drapery

Chapter 26: Sharpshooters

It is early morning in Leicester Square. The corruption and depravity of those living there is described.

At breakfast Phil Squod and his master, Mr George, discuss the 'country'. George remembers his early days as a country boy with evident longings. Phil is giving him a depressing autobiographical report: at the age of eight, he left the parish workhouse to follow a tinker, who later died of drink. Phil inherited that tinker's business, but his ugly looks, caused by burns and a serious accident, made him an outsider. Mr George found him, crippled and walking on two sticks, and brought him to the shooting gallery.

They have unexpected visitors: old Mr Smallweed is carried into the room, accompanied by his grand-daughter, Judith. Smallweed is frightened of Phil, and George bids him go. Old Smallweed tells George that Richard has had debts with him, but friends of Richard's paid for them. Smallweed is ready to squeeze more money out of the young man.

The purpose of his visit, however, is to get a sample of Captain Hawdon's writing from George for a lawyer in the city, who would like to compare it with some document he possesses. He talks George into accompanying him to that lawyer.

NOTES AND GLOSSARY:

Gentlemen of the green baize roads: swindlers at the card table

turn-ups: fights

the fifth of November: the capture of Guy Fawkes, one of the conspirators in the Gunpowder Plot, on 5 November 1605, is celebrated every year

paviour's rammer: tool used by pavement-makers to ram in the stones

---

Chapter 27: More Old Soldiers Than One

At Lincoln's Inn Fields, George, Mr Smallweed and Judy wait for Mr Tulkinghorn in the lawyer's great room. George's interest is roused by a box carrying the name of 'Dedlock'. Mr Tulkinghorn arrives. He is ready to offer George some money for anything written by Captain Hawdon. He then shows George the affidavit (see Chapter 2). George stays aloof, saying that 'he would rather have nothing to do with this'.

Before producing any such document George wants to consult one of his military friends. Old Smallweed, who has watched George put a paper in his pocket (see Chapter 26), cannot control his anger.

George goes to see his friend Matthew Bagnet, who lives out in the suburbs, where he keeps a modest musician's shop. He assures Mrs Bagnet that he will not lure her husband away, and plays with the little girls Quebec and Malta (called, in the family, after their barracks birthplaces). Although George enjoys the good-natured homeliness of the Bagnet household, he has grown thoughtful. Presently Mr Bagnet and his son Woolwich come home. Bluffy, as the children call Mr

George, is invited for dinner. Advice is given after the meal. George states his case and it is Mrs Bagnet who replies: George should not get involved in an affair he does not understand.

After slipping a shilling to his godson, Woolwich, George returns to Lincoln's Inn Fields, rather late. He meets Mr Tulkinghorn and tells him that he is still 'in the same mind', that is, he will not produce any sample of writing. Mr Tulkinghorn is angry and he haughtily dismisses him, saying that he regrets having let a man into his house who offered shelter to Gridley, 'a threatening, murderous, dangerous fellow.' These very words are overheard and misapplied to George by a passing clerk. George leaves, his indignation roused by Mr Tulkinghorn.

NOTES AND GLOSSARY:

brass-bound: here, making no concessions

Chapter 28: The Ironmaster

It is cold and damp in Lincolnshire. Sir Leicester is surrounded by his cousins, Miss Volumnia Dedlock and the Honourable Bob Stables, both people 'that are likely to have done well enough in life if they could have overcome their cousinship'. Sir Leicester 'stays out' his cousins like a martyr.

Volumnia mentions Rosa, 'one of the prettiest girls' that she has ever seen. Rosa, we are informed by Lady Dedlock, is a 'discovery' of Mrs Rouncewell's.

Sir Leicester tells the family circle to their dismay that Mrs Rouncewell's son, an ironmaster, has been invited to go into Parliament.

Mr Rouncewell is at this very moment at Chesney Wold on a brief visit to his mother; he has also asked in a well formulated note for an interview with Sir Leicester and Lady Dedlock.

The ironmaster comes when the cousins have retired. He does not mind his son getting engaged to Rosa, although he does not even know her, but he accepts the engagement on condition that Rosa does not remain at Chesney Wold. He wants her to have a better education than the one that has been given her by the village school. If Rosa is not given leave to go, he will ask his son (Watt) to reconsider his inclinations. Sir Leicester is shocked and sees the very framework of society threatened. Above all he resents the self-assurance of Mr Rouncewell.

Lady Dedlock does care for Rosa; she asks her about her relationship with young Rouncewell, but does not want to let her go. She spends a lonely, desolate evening in her apartment. The Dedlock cousins are shocked when told about Mr Rouncewell's behaviour.

NOTES AND GLOSSARY:

mash: mixture of ground feeds for cattle

Chapter 29: The Young Man

Chesney Wold is locked up, and the Dedlocks are in London. Mr Tulkinghorn is a frequent visitor, though Lady Dedlock is afraid of him.

A servant announces 'the young man of the name of Guppy', to Lady Dedlock. Sir Leicester, who has just been reading aloud a tedious newspaper article, is irritated, but as Lady Dedlock agrees to receive the young man, he gallantly withdraws.

Guppy introduces himself by telling Lady Dedlock that he works with Kenge and Carboy, but that he is also acquainted with Mr Tulkinghorn. He then comes to the point: does Lady Dedlock know a young person of the name of Esther Summerson? Did not the resemblance between her ladyship and Miss Summerson come to her notice? He confesses that he 'was knocked over' by that resemblance, when visiting Chesney Wold and seeing a portrait of Lady Dedlock.

Guppy glances at some notes he has made, and goes on. As Miss Summerson's image is imprinted on his heart, he could not but take an interest in her affairs. He cannot ignore an opportunity to put forward any claim Miss Summerson may have in the Jarndyce care, since it would further his own cause with her. So he has come to know a servant, now a Mrs Chadband, who used to work for Miss Barbary, who had Esther Summerson in her charge before Esther came into Mr Jarndyce's care. This former servant has told Guppy that Esther's real name is Hawdon. Lady Dedlock, who until now has been haughty and detached, cannot hide her shock.

Guppy now reveals that the law-writer at Krook's house was named Hawdon and that he, Guppy, knows all about her ladyship's having been guided by poor Jo to that dead man's grave. Furthermore Hawdon left a bundle of letters which Guppy will receive the following evening. Lady Dedlock is not very encouraging, when Guppy asks her whether he shall bring those letters. Still, he may do so. Guppy does not want to be paid for the letters. When he has left, Lady Dedlock weeps in her room for her child, who, her sister had told her, had died in the first hours of life.

NOTES AND GLOSSARY:
holland: a kind of plain, coarse linen
trumpet-tongued: compare Shakespeare's *Macbeth*, I.7.19

Chapter 30: Esther's Narrative

Mrs Woodcourt, Allan's mother, comes to Bleak House for a few days. She still harps on the importance of pedigree and tells Esther that her son is fickleness itself, as far as women are concerned. She tries to make

Esther forget Allan and tells her that Esther will, she thinks, one day marry a rich gentleman, considerably older than herself. Esther is left feeling uncomfortable.

Caddy comes down to ask Esther and Ada to be her bridesmaids. She is going to marry Prince within a month. Her father has gone through bankruptcy and has befriended Mr Turveydrop senior in the meantime. She and Prince are going to stay with Prince's father. Mr Jellyby will be with them, too, and perhaps even Peepy. Caddy's mother does not take any interest in the marriage preparations; she says that Caddy 'might have been equipped for Africa' at half the cost.

Esther, Ada and Charley busy themselves over preparing bridal clothes for their friend. Mr Jellyby, ashamed and forlorn in his messy lodgings, utters his longest speech: 'Never have a mission, my dear child'.

The wedding takes place, followed by a plain wedding breakfast. Mr Jarndyce and the Pardiggles are also among the guests. While people are all selfishly talking about their own problems, Esther and Mr Jarndyce try to make the feast as agreeable as possible.

Caddy and Prince leave for a week at Gravesend. Mrs Jellyby is indifferent; but her husband is very moved. Mr Turveydrop generously insists that the young couple stay with him. Esther and Ada return to Bleak House with their guardian who says that the wind is not in the east, despite the barely auspicious marriage feast, for 'wherever Dame Durden went, there was sunshine and summer air'.

NOTES AND GLOSSARY:

the Gazette:	an official journal, which publishes, among other things, the names of bankrupts
duets:	musical compositions for two performers
blacklead:	graphite

Chapter 31: Nurse and Patient (*Esther's narrative*)

Esther is tutoring Charley, her maid, who is having difficulty learning to write. Charley tells her mistress that Jenny and her friend, Liz, are in the neighbourhood again and that they are looking after a very sick orphan boy.

Esther accompanies Charley to the miserable lodgings (see Chapter 8) and notices that the place has a very close, 'very peculiar smell'. The boy whom they meet, Jo, is shaking with fever. He is much startled at Esther's veiled appearance. He does not want to be taken to the 'berryin' ground' on any account. Charley quietens him. Jo finally explains that he was running away from Mrs Snagsby, that he has been on the run ever since 't'other lady' gave him a sovereign. Liz has been out to find some proper refuge for the boy, but has been unsuccessful. Jo must leave the shabby hovel now, as Jenny's drunken husband is coming home. Jo shuffles out of the brickmaker's house, but Charley and Esther take him to Bleak House. Jo is quite confused: Are there *three* ladies who are much alike, 't'other one, the forenner [foreigner] and Esther'?

Mr Jarndyce puts Jo in the 'wholesome' loft, though Skimpole objects that there is a bad fever about the boy and he should be turned out.

Jo leaves his loft however and vanishes, and after a vain five-days' search Charley falls ill with a fever. Esther insists that Charley and herself should be isolated from the rest of the household. Charley is on the point of dying, but she recovers. Esther has been infected and will now be nursed by Charley. Esther tells her little maid that no one, not even Ada, is allowed to see her. She calls Charley to her bed and asks her to touch her, for 'I am blind'.

NOTES AND GLOSSARY:

a song about a Peasant boy: a song by John Parry (1776–1851)

negus: beverage of hot water, wine, sugar, lemon and nutmeg

Chapter 32: The Appointed Time

It is night in Lincoln's Inn. Singing and laughter come from the Sol's Arms, but people in the neighbouring courts find the atmosphere oppressive and close. Mr Weevle (Jobling, Krook's new lodger) and Mr Snagsby, both restless, meet outside the rag-and-bottle shop. Both are troubled by some unpleasant smell which seems to taint the whole neighbourhood. Mr Snagsby mentions the dead scrivener again and goes back to his shop before his wife starts looking for him. In fact, she has already followed him.

Guppy stealthily appears and is led to Weevle's room. Conversation is lagging, while Guppy admires Lady Dedlock's portrait. After some quarrelsome talk they come to the purpose of their meeting; they are to be given a bundle of letters by Krook at twelve o'clock. These letters were probably written by a lady. The name of Hawdon, which Krook managed to copy, is mentioned.

A greasy omnipresent soot disturbs their talk. Krook is to be tricked out of his papers by being given a dummy packet of letters. Bart Smallweed will not be let into the secret. Some disgusting oily substance, 'with some natural repulsion in it', is dripping from the window-sill. At the appointed time, St Paul's strikes twelve, Weevle goes down to Krook's room. He returns at once, aghast. Krook is not there, but his room is filled with oil and soot and a burning smell.

Guppy accompanies him now. Krook has been charred to death, the

papers are nothing but tinder, the only living being in the room is the
disquieting cat. Krook has 'died the death of all Lord Chancellors in all
Courts, and of all authorities – where false pretences are made'. It is the
death of 'spontaneous combustion', the only suitable form of dying for
such a person.

NOTES AND GLOSSARY:

The Appointed Time: for the title of this chapter see the Bible, Job 7:1
Argus: a mythical monster with a hundred eyes
Yorick: the king's (dead) jester in Shakespeare's *Hamlet*
the gruff line: the bass part
I am in the Downs: I feel depressed
Bogey: a monstrous imaginary figure used in threatening children
spontaneous combustion: there were polemics in the papers about the possibility of spontaneous combustion after the publication of this chapter. Dickens was offended and felt the need to justify himself (see Author's Preface). This implausibility does not diminish the symbolic value of Krook's death

Chapter 33: Interlopers

Chancery Lane is in a state of uproar. Weevle and Guppy are being
offered drinks at the Sol's Arms, as they are attracting customers.

Mr Snagsby turns up at break of day, and so does his 'little woman'.
Mrs Snagsby is so suspicious that her husband starts doubting whether
he 'may not for some inconceivable part be responsible for Krook's
death'.

Guppy and Weevle discuss their points of evidence to be given at the
inquest. They agree that they met at the rag-and-bottle shop in order to
explain some piece of writing to the illiterate Krook. Although Guppy
would like his friend to keep his room, Weevle refuses. He is horrified.

The Smallweeds arrive by coach. Krook was Mrs Smallweed's
brother, and they have now come to look after 'the property'. Mr
Tulkinghorn is their solicitor and he is answerable for everything being
correctly handled. A coffin has been ordered by Grandpa Smallweed,
though there is 'so little to put in it'.

Guppy makes a call on Lady Dedlock, who is about to leave for a
dinner-party. Guppy can merely tell her that he has not been able to get
the papers. She dismisses him and he is told not to call again. On his
leaving he meets Mr Tulkinghorn. Tulkinghorn knows Guppy, and the
old lawyer and Lady Dedlock look at one another for a brief moment
with sharp suspicion.

NOTES AND GLOSSARY:

interlopers:	intruders
tissue-paper:	thin paper to make multiple copies
cloves:	spice used in a hot punch
Phoenix:	the Phoenix was the emblem of a fire-insurance company
shrub:	punch made of rum, fruit rind, fruit juice and sugar
Windsor arm-chair:	a kind of wooden chair, usually with a high back
Philosophical Transactions:	see Dickens's Preface
six-footer:	coffin

Chapter 34: A Turn of the Screw

George is summoned by old Mr Smallweed to pay roughly one hundred pounds, a bill drawn on him by his friend Matthew Bagnet. Phil Squod darkly hints at mischief coming from all this. An understanding that the bill is to be renewed is apparently no longer valid. Mr and Mrs Bagnet quite unexpectedly turn up at the shooting gallery to have the new bill signed. George has to tell them about Smallweed's demands. Having overcome her shock (a threat to the security would ruin the Bagnets) Mrs Bagnet, who speaks for her husband, is ready 'to forget and to forgive', although George should not have taken the shooting gallery without the appropriate means.

Mr Bagnet and George go to see Grandpa Smallweed, who, after a brief discussion, tells George that he is ready 'to smash him', that is, he will not yield at all. The claimant is Mr Tulkinghorn, old Mr Smallweed's friend in the city. They are thrown out of the house and proceed to the old lawyer's. They wait patiently at Tulkinghorn's office. The lawyer is apparently very busy. Old Mrs Rouncewell leaves his office; she at once starts a friendly conversation with them, as they remind her of her lost soldier son.

Finally admitted, George is refused any help by Tulkinghorn whatsoever until, however reluctantly, he agrees to produce that sample of writing. Tulkinghorn now agrees to replace the financial matter 'on its old footing', furthermore the Bagnets will not be troubled any more, until 'George has been proceeded against to the utmost.'

George has lunch at the Bagnets'. The atmosphere is hearty and warm as usual, though George is in very low spirits.

NOTES AND GLOSSARY:

whitewashing:	here, declaring himself bankrupt
lignum vitae:	(*Latin*, the wood of life) a type of hard wood from the West Indies
in close order:	(*military*) closed up

Chapter 35: Esther's Narrative

Esther is seriously ill; suffering from nightmares, she sees herself 'labouring up colossal staircases'. Her eyesight is, however, restored to her. Ada, though bitterly disappointed, has not been allowed to nurse her. When she feels a little better Charley prepares a tea-party for the two of them and has the looking-glass removed.

Her guardian can now enter the sick-room, too. He has stayed as trustworthy and loving as ever and brings messages from Caddy and Ada – and Richard, who writes cold, haughty letters, convinced as he is by his legal investigations that Mr Jarndyce cannot be trusted in the Cause. Rick has been spoilt by the Jarndyce and Jarndyce suit, 'the curtain of his cradle', as Esther's guardian puts it.

Trying to accustom herself and her acquaintances, especially Ada, to her scarred face Esther accepts an invitation from Mr Boythorn.

Miss Flite has walked all the way to pay a sick-bed visit. She tells Esther that on her way she met Jenny, the brickmaker's wife, who told her that a 'lady with a veil' had come to see her, and had taken away the very handkerchief Esther had used to cover the dead baby's face (Chapter 8). Esther thinks it might have been Caddy, and does not think any more about the incident.

Miss Flite confides to her that although most of her relatives have died expecting a Judgement, she still feels mysteriously and cruelly attracted to Chancery. She fears that she may have noticed the same corrosive signs in Richard. Allan Woodcourt, meanwhile, has been shipwrecked in the Far East and behaved most heroically. Miss Flite gives Esther a newspaper clipping telling her all about it.

Esther confides to the reader her love for Allan Woodcourt, and her relief that, since nothing had been said between them, she need never feel the pangs of a rupture now, because she is fully convinced that Dr Woodcourt would now no longer be attracted to her, with her altered looks.

NOTES AND GLOSSARY:

tambour work: embroidery done on a circular frame

Chapter 36: Chesney Wold (*Esther's narrative*)

Charley and Esther, accompanied by Mr Jarndyce, set off for Mr Boythorn's house in Lincolnshire. Esther enjoys the scenery and at last musters the courage to look at herself in a mirror. She has very much changed, but quietly accepts that change. She also resolves to keep Allan Woodcourt's flowers which she had carefully dried and put in a book.

Her guardian has returned to Bleak House with a letter for Ada, who will join Esther in a week. Esther is accepted by the villagers and comes to like the grounds of Chesney Wold. Here, one day, she meets Lady Dedlock, who is supposed to be in London. Lady Dedlock asks her to send Charley home. She has that handkerchief with her that Esther left with Jenny's dead child. Lady Dedlock falls on her knees in front of Esther with the words 'O my child, my child, I am your wicked and unhappy mother! O try to forgive me!'

She tells Esther that she was nearly crazy with anxiety during her illness, but she also insists on keeping her secret safe. Tulkinghorn, she is fully aware, may know about her, though her husband does not suspect anything.

Shocked and stunned, Esther at last manages to part from her mother and returns to Boythorn's. There she reads the letter Lady Dedlock has given her. She now knows that her mother did not abandon her; Lady Dedlock was convinced that her child had 'never breathed – had been buried – had never borne a name'.

Esther now feels guilty that she should have brought disaster to Lady Dedlock and to her family. In the evening, while walking along the Ghost's Walk, she identifies her own steps with those that can be heard on the flagged stones and are supposed to bring calamity upon the house.

The chapter ends with Esther waiting for Ada to come and see her for the first time since her recovery. Ada's feelings are unaltered and she is still the same reliable friend.

NOTES AND GLOSSARY:

Stubbs: Esther's pony is named after a well-known English painter of horses, George Stubbs (1724–1806)

Chapter 37: Jarndyce and Jarndyce (*Esther's narrative*)

Esther, Ada and Charley are now to stay a month at Mr Boythorn's. Esther, because her secret is not only hers, has to keep it even from Ada, though she has some difficulty in doing so.

One evening Charley tells her young mistress that she is 'wanted at the Dedlock Arms' by a gentleman. This gentleman turns out to be Richard, who is not at all shocked by her changed appearance. He tells Esther that he is on leave and that they 'are beginning to spin along with that old suit'. Harold Skimpole, who has now become Richard's crony, joins them. In Esther's opinion, Richard could not have possibly chosen a worse friend.

They go to Boythorn's house. Richard will respect Mr Jarndyce's injunction and not renew his engagement (see Chapter 24). Skimpole is still very much the same man, relying on 'somebody' to bail him out.

During a walk with Esther the following day Richard tells her that he is still suspicious of John Jarndyce: if the suit 'taints everybody . . . why should *he* escape?' Richard tries to justify his present behaviour and wants Esther to explain his conduct to Ada. He is going to make the case 'the object of his life'. We are also told that he is in debt again.

Ada now writes a letter to Richard, urging him to desist from his disastrous course. Esther's advice, Ada writes, has been perfectly sound; she herself will be ready to follow him, no matter how modest his fortune may be. Skimpole, on Esther's entreaties, is not willing to talk good sense with Richard; worse, he has even accepted a bribe from Vholes, a lawyer, in order to introduce Richard to him.

Vholes has come to Lincolnshire to inform Richard that the cause will be up before the Court next day. Richard hurries off to London the following morning, although his presence at the Court, according to Vholes, will not be of any use.

Ada insists that she will stay with Richard, no matter what happens.

NOTES AND GLOSSARY:

adage about little pitchers: a reference to a proverbial saying, 'little pitchers have large ears', that is, children hear very well

cage: prison

I am not like the starling: Skimpole alludes to a caged starling in Laurence Sterne's (1713–68) *A Sentimental Journey*

Chapter 38: A Struggle (*Esther's narrative*)

Her health and strength being perfectly restored, Esther returns to Bleak House, where she immediately resumes her housekeeping. A couple of days later, she travels to London, a visit to Caddy being the pretext, though in reality she is induced by something in Lady Dedlock's letter.

She finds Caddy and her husband happily living together, that is, staying in two modest rooms, with Caddy's father-in-law having taken over the best part of the lodgings. Caddy is training to become a dancing-mistress; she has to look after four young apprentices as well. Peepy has settled down with them and has become old Mr Turveydrop's errand-boy.

The main purpose of the trip to London, however, is a visit to the Old Street Road, to the Guppys', where Esther now goes, accompanied by Caddy. Mrs Guppy is present as well, smiling waggishly, obviously misunderstanding the purpose of Esther's visit.

Esther asks to be allowed to speak with young Guppy alone. She lifts her veil and Guppy is acutely embarrassed, even appalled, at what he thinks is Esther's impending declaration that she is going to accept his offer of marriage. Esther reassures him and tells him now about the purpose of her visit: though Guppy might be able to explore and unfold some of Esther's private history, she wants him to stop his investigations. Guppy accepts, but on Esther's leaving he makes her give an absurdly full and formal declaration, with Caddy as a witness, that she never intended to marry him.

NOTES AND GLOSSARY:

Mews:	stables
sweeps:	chimney-sweeps
kit:	small, narrow violin

Chapter 39: Attorney and Client

Mr Vholes's shabby and dingy legal bearings in Symond's Inn, Chancery Lane, are described. Mr Vholes is a most 'respectable' man, 'making hay of the grass which is flesh' for his three daughters and his father. He has understood that the one great principle of English law is to make business for itself and he acts accordingly. Any change in the legal practice would bring serious damage to a whole class of practitioners, among whom Mr Vholes is mentioned in some Parliamentary minutes on the subject as being 'a *most* respectable man'; in other words, nothing will ever be changed.

Richard, now at Vholes's office, has grown very impatient. He feels like Ixion bound to the wheel, whereas Mr Vholes tries to impart some of his own 'insensibility' to his disappointed young client. Mr Vholes asks for twenty pounds on account, and Richard readily writes the draft; it is in fact an advance on his next allowance as a Chancery ward. Richard leaves the office, centring his disappointment on the embodiment of his suspicions, John Jarndyce.

Guppy and Weevle watch Richard leaving Symond's Inn, a case of 'smouldering combustion', according to Weevle. Both are on their way to Krook's to remove Weevle's belongings. Guppy thinks that the letters might have escaped the fire. If Weevle were to find them, he ought to burn them, because Guppy has no interest in them any more; his image as he says, 'is shattered', 'his idol laid low'.

The Smallweed family is searching the house for hidden or forgotten objects of value. Guppy and Weevle are admitted. To Guppy's discomfiture, Tulkinghorn is present as well. Tulkinghorn compliments him for having free admission to great houses.

When they take down the Galaxy Gallery of aristocratic portraits, Tulkinghorn says of the Lady Dedlock portrait that 'it wants force of character'. Guppy repeats that whatever interesting contacts he may have had with aristocracy are severed now, 'shattered' like his idol.

NOTES AND GLOSSARY:

hatchment:	panel with the coat of arms of a deceased person
blue minutes:	notes recorded on blue official paper
Ixion:	in Greek mythology, he was bound to an ever-revolving wheel of fire in Hades
Tattoo:	a rapid, rhythmic drumming or rapping; the 'Devil's Tattoo' is a rapping betraying impatience
the Monument:	a column commemorating the Great Fire of London of 1666
pantaloons:	close-fitting trousers
swanlike:	perfect

Chapter 40: National and Domestic

'Coodle' has gone, 'Doodle' has not come yet: it is pre-election time, and England has been without a government for some weeks. As Sir Leicester is coming back to Chesney Wold, Mrs Rouncewell prepares the house. Thomas, a groom, arrives and warns Mrs Rouncewell that Lady Dedlock does not feel well.

Sir Leicester and Lady Dedlock have arrived with their 'largest retinue'. The cousins have come as well. Volumnia discusses politics with Sir Leicester. Both are irritated that the middle class, a 'faction' only, should prove rebellious. Sir Leicester wants to 'observe a crushing aspect' towards his cousin, in order to prevent her from analysing the financial expenses of his party that might be connected with bribery.

Volumnia remarks, all of a sudden, that Mr Tulkinghorn must be quite busy. At the mentioning of this name Lady Dedlock seems to take a very slight interest in the conversation. Presently Tulkinghorn is announced. Volumnia is charmed, as he is her 'idol'. A gun fired close by startles everyone. Lady Dedlock thinks a rat has been shot.

Tulkinghorn enters. Lady Dedlock prefers the twilight and the 'Mercuries' take their lamps away again. Tulkinghorn tells Sir Leicester that he is beaten 'out of all reason'. Mr Rouncewell, he informs the Dedlocks, was very active against the Conservatives in this election, so was his son. Sir Leicester advises Lady Dedlock to keep Rosa away from 'such dangerous hands', as young Rouncewell is Rosa's suitor.

Tulkinghorn, however, remarks that, in their way, people such as the Rouncewells are very proud. He then proceeds to tell the story of 'a friend of Mr Rouncewell', whose daughter was the favourite maid of some great lady. This lady had many years ago been engaged to a merry rake, a young captain. She never married him, though she gave birth to his child. She later married somebody of Sir Leicester's station in life. Although of a very firm character, she was unable to keep her secret; through an imprudence on her own part her story was disclosed. The point of Mr Tulkinghorn's story is, however, that Mr Rouncewell's friend had his daughter removed from the patronage of such a lady.

NOTES AND GLOSSARY:

in the forms of sovereigns and beer: see Carlyle's text in Literary background and other influences, p. 12

pilot fish: small fish that swims in company with a shark

auriferous: literally, carrying gold

auriferous and malty shower: distribution of money and beer (in order to buy votes)

basilisk: legendary reptile with fatal breath and glance

kid gloves: gloves made of kid leather

sash: band worn round the waist

tucker: piece of cloth or lace in the neckline of a dress

Freemason: member of a major secret fraternal society; short aprons and trowels are the attributes of freemasons

---

Chapter 41: In Mr Tulkinghorn's Room

Mr Tulkinghorn is in his turret-room, 'sedately satisfied'. Lady Dedlock has been watching him from the corridor; she now enters. Her immediate question is, 'why have you told my story to so many persons?' Mr Tulkinghorn calmly tells her that he thought it his duty to inform Lady Dedlock that he was aware of her secret. At the same time he assures her that her secret has not yet been publicly divulged, and that Rosa has not yet been affected by it.

Lady Dedlock is ready to sign any confession if she can thereby release her husband from his present condition and divert any harm from Rosa. In fact, she charges Tulkinghorn to tell Chesney Wold that she is lost to the world. Tulkinghorn persuades her to stay, out of consideration for Sir Leicester, insisting all the time on his own duties towards the baronet. Is Lady Dedlock therefore to go on hiding her guilt? Yes, Tulkinghorn says, he will not take any steps towards disclosure without forewarning her.

Lady Dedlock leaves the turret-chamber in the small hours with the sun rising over this 'happy home in Lincolnshire'.

Chapter 42: In Mr Tulkinghorn's Chambers

Mr Tulkinghorn is back in his London quarters at Lincoln's Inn Fields. At his door he is met by Snagsby, who is very upset as his wife is having 'such fits of jealousy' because of Mademoiselle Hortense (see Chapter 22). She is haunting his shop and disturbing his wife and, particularly, Guster, who is prone to fits. Tulkinghorn tells Snagsby to send Hortense to him.

The Frenchwoman, however, turns up unexpectedly at his lodgings when Tulkinghorn is on the point of fetching one of his cobwebbed bottles of port. She throws away the two sovereigns that she was given, when she showed herself to Jo in Lady Dedlock's clothes (see Chapter 22). She is filled with rancour and bent on harming Lady Dedlock, whose service she has had to leave. Tulkinghorn threatens to have her jailed if she is to importune Snagsby or himself again. Hortense withdraws with a threatening whisper: 'I will prove you'. Tulkinghorn can at last enjoy his port.

NOTES AND GLOSSARY:

'I never had an idea of a foreign female . . . earrings': Mr Snagsby refers to
    street-peddlars and gipsies

Chapter 43: Esther's Narrative

Esther is deeply troubled by her mother's secret, and she fears that her 'mere existence' might betray her as being Lady Dedlock's illegitimate child.

Ada and Esther often discuss Richard with their guardian. Richard is still in his stubborn and suspicious mood. Esther is sceptical about Skimpole's influence on Richard. John Jarndyce, obviously annoyed, agrees to pay a visit to Skimpole, who is a perfectly harmless person in his eyes. They find Skimpole in a very neglected house, almost empty of furniture. 'Richard is full of poetry,' he tells his visitors, 'I love him'. Jarndyce warns Skimpole not to borrow money from Richard again. Skimpole is astonished, telling his visitors that he thought Richard was immensely rich. His three daughters, 'Beauty', 'Sentiment' and 'Comedy', are introduced. John Jarndyce discreetly leaves some money with Mrs Skimpole.

As his 'amiability' has already been tried by a creditor this morning, Skimpole will join his friends, who return to Bleak House. He doesn't bother about his family at all. He manages to cheer up Mr Jarndyce on their way home.

An unexpected visitor is announced: Sir Leicester Dedlock. He comes to apologise for the unfriendly atmosphere they met with when attempting to visit Chesney Wold. He feels particularly sorry that a gentleman with 'a cultivated taste for the Fine Arts' should not have been able to see the family portraits. This gentleman turns out to have been Skimpole, who during the ensuing conversation, is shown as a true sycophant, ready to slight even Boythorn.

Esther withdraws to her room in order to recover her self-command. She decides to seek her guardian's advice; late at night she asks him whether he still remembers Lady Dedlock mentioning having had a sister, whom Mr Jarndyce must have known (see Chapter 18).

The two women 'had gone their several ways'. Her guardian tells her that this sister was the very woman Boythorn had hoped to marry, but that she had refused him, probably because of that quarrel with her sister. She told Boythorn in a letter that 'she died to him'. Esther must now tell her guardian that this sister is her 'first remembrance'. Mr Jarndyce stays very calm and gently comforts her, thereby making Esther still more devoted to him.

NOTES AND GLOSSARY:

the Polygon: a run-down block of late eighteenth-century houses. Young Charles Dickens lived there in the 1820s

poor Spanish refugees: Spanish exiles had come to live in that part of London

nectarine: peach-like fruit

barcaroles: songs commonly sung by Venetian gondoliers

old Verulam wall: remains of the walls of a city, called Verulamium in Roman times (near St Albans)

Chapter 44: The Letter and the Answer (*Esther's narrative*)

The next day Mr Jarndyce gives further advice to Esther concerning her mother's secret: she need not have any personal guilt, though Mr Jarndyce feels that Tulkinghorn may be a dangerous man. Guppy can be trusted, the French maid is less reassuring.

Mr Jarndyce still wants to broach a difficult subject. He is therefore going to put it down in a letter that Charley is to fetch for Esther in a week's time.

In this letter John Jarndyce asks Esther to marry him, and to become mistress of Bleak House. It is an honest letter, carefully analysing the problems arising from the difference in their ages. Mr Jarndyce does not mention Esther's disfigurement or her social origins at all.

Esther feels thankful, even happy, but she cries, because something hard to define for her at this very moment seems to be lost for ever.

She resolves to be cheerful, though she burns the now dried flowers given to her by Allan Woodcourt. Esther finds it difficult to write down a 'good' answer for her guardian. When Skimpole has left again, she goes to find Mr Jarndyce and kisses him. She thus agrees to become the mistress of Bleak House. Ada is not let into the secret.

Chapter 45: In Trust (*Esther's narrative*)

Mr Vholes comes to Bleak House. Esther is called to Mr Jarndyce's study and is told by Mr Vholes that Richard's liabilities are such that he may be in danger of losing his army commission. Esther at once resolves to travel down to Deal, where Richard is stationed, to discuss matters with him, as he is still quite unwilling to accept any form of help from Mr Jarndyce.

Taking Charley with her, she travels to Deal by night. She has two letters with her, one from Mr Jarndyce, the other from Ada. They find Deal a dreary place, but cheer up after they have refreshed themselves at a comfortable hotel. They watch the ships, among them an Indiaman, the attraction of the harbour.

Esther finds Richard in plain clothes at his barracks, in very disorderly surroundings, looking wild and haggard (for the first time Esther hints at Richard's possible early death).

His welcome though is cheerful and boyish again; he makes it quite clear that he will not even talk about John Jarndyce, but that he will devote all his efforts to the cause. Ada's letter moves him. She is ready to offer him her own inheritance, an amount equal to the one he has wasted. Richard does not accept this. He has finished with the army, and, blindly relying on Vholes, accompanies Esther to London.

Returning to their hotel Esther and Charley meet some of the officers who have just left the Indiaman. Flushed, Esther hurries to her room. She has just recognised Allan Woodcourt and does not want him to see her altered looks. These officers, however, will lodge at her hotel and Esther, rather on impulse, sends a card to Allan, who comes to see her at once. Allan behaves with the utmost sensitivity. He has not been lucky in India and will not return. Richard greets him, and although he is again in one of his exuberant moods Allan notices that something is wrong, that he is both weary and desperate. Esther asks Allan to befriend Richard in London. Allan gladly accepts the charge.

NOTES AND GLOSSARY:

Flora: Roman goddess of flowers
the Downs: here, part of the English Channel off the east coast of Kent

---

Chapter 46: Stop Him!

'Darkness rests upon Tom-all-Alone's'. Ominously we are told that its corruption will spread to and infect other places as well. Dr Woodcourt walks down its main street, 'a stagnant channel of mud', where he finds the brickmaker's wife, Jenny, huddled on a doorstep. He dresses an ugly bruise on her forehead. On leaving her he passes a boy whom he seems to remember vaguely. The brickmaker's wife shouts 'Stop him', rushing after the youth. Allan brings him to bay in a dead alley and is told by the poor woman that this is Jo, who infected Esther with smallpox. Jo is mortified but steadfastly refuses to reveal anything of his whereabouts in the meantime. He will eventually disclose that he was 'took' by somebody (Inspector Bucket), of whom he seems to be afraid, and brought to a hospital. At his release he was told 'to tramp about'. As he is obviously deadly ill Allan will try to find him some decent lodgings.

NOTES AND GLOSSARY:
I dusn't, I dustn't: I dare not

Chapter 47: Jo's Will

Allan finds it strange that it is more difficult to find a home for a human being than for an unowned dog. Jo is so miserable that he is beyond hunger. Having sipped some wine he recovers slightly and is able to tell Allan about the lady in the veil and all the consequences of that encounter. Allan thinks of lodging Jo at Miss Flite's, but the rag-and-bottle shop is shut up; the unfriendly Judy Smallweed rules there now. Miss Flite lives at Mrs Blinder's (see Chapter 15) and brings them to 'General George'. At the shooting gallery Allan explains to George that Jo must be kept away from Bucket the detective; Mr Jarndyce and Esther should, however, know of Jo's whereabouts. George readily offers hospitality to Jo, insisting that he would do anything, at any time, that might please Miss Summerson. Allan assures him that Jo does not carry any infectious disease, but he must also know that Jo is likely to die soon. This only increases George's readiness for hospitality and he offers him a cabin at the end of his gallery. Phil Squod, found in the gutter as a baby, will look after him. George tells Allan that the place to which Jo was brought must have been Tulkinghorn's rooms in Lincoln's Inn Fields and that Tulkinghorn himself is 'a confoundedly bad and slow-torturing kind of man'. Allan leaves and soon returns with John Jarndyce. Jo is getting weaker and weaker and as he mentions 'Sangsby' [Snagsby] Allan decides to call on the law-stationer. Mr Snagsby visits Jo that evening, and promises that he will write in very large letters that Jo 'is sorry to have done it', that is, to have infected Esther.

Jo's end is approaching fast. He wants to be buried in that same shabby 'berryin ground . . . where they laid him as was very good to me' (Captain Hawdon, or 'Nemo').

NOTES AND GLOSSARY:

Divan:	Oriental courtroom
. . . drum-head:	summary court-martial that tries offences on the battlefield, the drum-head was used as a table
skins:	parchments
engrosser:	one who copies legal documents in a large, clear hand

Chapter 48: Closing In

The guests have departed from Chesney Wold and the Dedlocks are in London again. Lady Dedlock, haughtier than ever before, informs Rosa that she has written to ask Mr Rouncewell, her prospective father-in-law, to come and take her away. She is going to dismiss her for her, Rosa's, own sake.

Mr Rouncewell is announced. Lady Dedlock goes to the library to inform her husband. She finds him in conversation with Tulkinghorn. Lady Dedlock earnestly wants to know whether young Rouncewell's fancy is still caught by Rosa. If so, Rosa had better leave Chesney Wold. Sir Leicester pompously objects that Rosa has been very lucky to have attracted the notice of so eminent a lady; he cannot understand that Rosa should be dismissed because she attracted Mr Rouncewell's son, or that the young girl could possibly prefer to live with the ironmaster's family. Rouncewell is then sent for. He is disdainful, though polite, and leaves with Rosa.

The following day, Mr Tulkinghorn, who is working in Sir Leicester's library, asks if he might see Lady Dedlock. He tells her that their mutual agreement has been broken (see Chapter 41), an agreement consisting in Lady Dedlock's acquiescence in strictly following her usual way of life without any change whatsoever. This is Tulkinghorn's way of telling Lady Dedlock 'that things are closing in'. He leaves, and walks home. Lady Dedlock goes out for a walk.

At home, Tulkinghorn fetches a bottle of port. A shot disturbs the few people that are still about in Lincoln's Inn Fields. Early in the morning, when cleaners come to his lodgings, the painted Roman soldier's finger points to Tulkinghorn, dead, shot through the heart.

NOTES AND GLOSSARY:

inconvenient women: Sir Leicester's 'debilitated cousin' seems to be thinking of Lady Macbeth sleepwalking (Shakespeare, *Macbeth*, V.1)

Chancery pipes have no stop: a traditional pipe has holes or 'stops'

Chapter 49: Dutiful Friendship

In a Pickwickian mood Dickens describes a birthday party at the Bagnets'. Matthew insists on ritualising Mrs Bagnet's birthday year after year; he will, as a surprise, prepare two fowls, 'triumphs of toughness'. George is also of the party, but he is not in his usual cheerful mood. Bucket turns up, apparently looking for a second-hand violoncello for an acquaintance, but despite his homely and good-natured talk, he closely scrutinises both people and place.

When George and Bucket leave, the detective suddenly pushes his

friend into the parlour of an inn. There he tells George that he is
suspected of having killed Tulkinghorn. Sir Leicester has offered a
reward. George is handcuffed and taken away.

NOTES AND GLOSSARY:
cross-grained: difficult to deal with
'Believe me . . .':   a popular song by Thomas Moore (1779–1852)
scratch: here, the starting-line in a race

Chapter 50: Esther's Narrative

Caddy, after giving birth to a very frail baby, has fallen seriously ill. She
appeals to Esther, who nurses her. She reports to her guardian, who
suggests that they send for Allan Woodcourt. Esther is confused and
notices that Ada still remembers the nosegay.

As it is Ada's twenty-first birthday, Esther discloses to her that she is
to become the mistress of Bleak House.

Esther looks after Caddy during the following eight weeks. The
visitors, Prince excepted, show their usual carelessness. Mrs Jellyby is
far more interested in Borrioboola-Gha than in her daughter's or
grandchild's health; old Mr Turveydrop, though fond of Peepy, still
insists on being the subject of many civilities.

Thanks to Allan's competent help Caddy recovers, and on Mr
Jarndyce's praising his talents Esther again notices that something
seems to weigh down on Ada, though she is reluctant to speak of it.

Chapter 51: Enlightened (*Esther's narrative*)

We move back a few weeks. Allan has been dutifully looking after
Richard. He saw Mr Vholes who hinted darkly that Richard would soon
need more money again. Richard lives next door to Vholes and on
Allan's suggestion Esther and Ada will visit him.

His lodgings are even shabbier than those at Deal and Ada now
confides to her friend that she married Richard two months ago and will
not leave him any more. Esther feels that she ought to protect Ada. Back
at Bleak House Esther feels lonely and depressed, when John Jarndyce
comes home (it is the day of Jo's death).

She tells him about Ada's marriage and she is somehow disappointed
that her guardian only says that Bleak House is 'thinning fast'. Has she
not lived up to his expectations?

Chapter 52: Obstinacy (*Esther's narrative*)

Allan breaks the news of Tulkinghorn's death to Esther and Mr
Jarndyce. Esther immediately thinks of her mother, whose potentially

most dangerous enemy has now disappeared. They are all convinced that George is innocent.

Allan has seen Phil Squod, who has told him that it was his master's main worry that his friends might no longer trust him.

Together they all set off to prison. George is cheered by their loyalty, but, to their surprise, he will not accept the help of any lawyer. Mr Jarndyce tries to explain to him that Gridley was the victim of the Court of Chancery, of Equity, but that his case will be tried in one of the courts of Common Law. It is all to no avail; George simply wants to be totally cleared.

Mr and Mrs Bagnet are now allowed into the cell. Mrs Bagnet has brought some food, and she signs to the others to leave her alone with George. As they go George says that a figure in a black-fringed cloak passed him on Mr Tulkinghorn's staircase on the night of the murder, which reminded him of Esther Summerson. Esther is profoundly disturbed.

Mrs Bagnet joins the group outside again. She knows how to help George: she knows that his old mother is still alive and living in Lincolnshire. She sets off on her own to fetch her.

NOTES AND GLOSSARY:

under remand: sent back to court for further instructions
Equity: see the notes on Law Courts, p. 8
an eight-and-forty pounder: a cannon that fired a missile of forty-eight pounds

---

Chapter 53: The Track

Mr Bucket visits all the places to which Tulkinghorn used to go. He is present at the funeral, watching from a coach. Sir Leicester is the only mourner actually present, though there is a whole row of empty coaches belonging to the peerage.

Bucket goes to the Dedlocks' house in London, which has almost become his own home now. The footman gives him another letter, the sixth so far. He opens it and reads the message written by the same hand: 'LADY DEDLOCK'.

Having had his dinner, Bucket is summoned to see Sir Leicester, whom he meets in the drawing-room. Volumnia and 'the debilitated cousin' are present as well. Sir Leicester is ready to go to any expense to have the case cleared. He insists that he is much indebted to the late Mr Tulkinghorn. Volumnia has grown very curious, but Bucket will not divulge anything. In his eyes, it is a 'beautiful case', nearly complete.

When leaving Bucket wheedles out some information concerning Lady Dedlock from the footman. Her ladyship goes out for dinner every day, he is told.

Lady Dedlock comes home, and is introduced to Bucket. When she
withdraws he comments on her ill looks. She suffers from headaches, he
is told, and often takes a walk at night. Bucket now 'remembers' that
Lady Dedlock left the house the night of the murder at half past nine.
She was wearing a black, fringed cloak. The footman confirms this.

NOTES AND GLOSSARY:

Herald's College: corporation supervising the use of coats of arms
three bereaved worms: three footmen dressed in mourning clothes
sacked depository of noble secrets: Tulkinghorn, the 'silent depository' of
                                     Chapter 2, is now 'sacked', that is, wrapped in a
                                     shroud
Blue Chamber: Bluebeard (in the story *Bluebeard*) has a forbidden
                                     room, the Blue Chamber, in which he keeps the
                                     corpses of his murdered wives
makes a leg: bows

Chapter 54: Springing a Mine

Having had a solid breakfast, Mr Bucket goes to meet Sir Leicester in the
library again. The baronet is a little late, suffering from an attack of gout
brought on by recent circumstances.

Bucket is careful to ensure that no one could possibly hear their
conversation, and he tells Sir Leicester that his case is now complete:
George is not the murderer; a woman committed the deed. When Bucket
tries to impart all the information he has, Sir Leicester objects to his
wife's name being mentioned. Bucket insists that this is impossible.

Sir Leicester trembles, and finds it difficult to control himself when he
is told that Tulkinghorn had some suspicions concerning Lady Dedlock.
These suspicions were aroused when her ladyship was interested in some
copyist's handwriting; they were confirmed when, dressed in her maid's
clothes, she visited the wretched grave of that man. Bucket now wants
the baronet to ask his lady whether she went to Lincoln's Inn Fields, in a
black, fringed mantle on the night of the murder, and whether she
passed 'the soldier' (Mr George) on Tulkinghorn's staircase. Sir
Leicester shows true dignity at all these painful revelations; at the same
time the first signs of a cerebral haemorrhage become noticeable, as he
has some difficulty when speaking.

He cannot understand why Tulkinghorn, whom he trusted so much,
should have kept the knowledge from him. Bucket suggests that
Tulkinghorn was probably ready to divulge Lady Dedlock's secret.

They are disturbed by some loud voices outside. Bucket admits old
Smallweed, Mr and Mrs Chadband and Mrs Snagsby into the library.
Smallweed is furious at no longer having the letters written by one
Honoria to her lover, Captain Hawdon. Smallweed had found those

letters and handed them to Tulkinghorn after having glanced through them. Bucket, however, produces the bundle of letters!

Smallweed and Chadband, each in his own way, are ready to accept money in exchange for their knowledge. Mrs Chadband (Miss Barbary's former maid Rachael) tells the assembly how she brought up Miss Hawdon (Esther). Finally Mrs Snagsby gives a confused account of her problems. They are dismissed, but Bucket recommends to Sir Leicester to 'buy them up'. Sir Leicester is now to watch the arrest of the true murderer, who happens to be in the house.

Hortense, Lady Dedlock's French servant-maid, is admitted. She is surprised at finding Sir Leicester and the inspector in the library. She had expected to find Lady Dedlock. Bucket, keeping a vigilant eye on Hortense, tells her and the baronet how he accepted her as his lodger, how she arranged an alibi by going to the theatre before and after the murder.

Bucket had told his wife to watch their guest all the time. Hortense was thus observed writing her anonymous letters, and even the weapon she had used could be recovered, thanks to the watchful Mrs Bucket. Bucket now handcuffs Hortense, who has been insolent and malicious throughout his revelations.

Sir Leicester Dedlock is left alone, old and sick, but unflinching in his loyalty and love towards his wife.

NOTES AND GLOSSARY:

to spring a mine: to operate a trap suddenly, to disclose unexpectedly
smalls: knee-breeches
mag: half penny
nobbiest: (*slang*) smartest, best
it begins to look like Queer Street: it looks as if there is going to be trouble

---

Chapter 55: Flight

We now move back twenty-four hours. The night before Hortense's arrest Mrs Rouncewell is brought to London by Mrs Bagnet. Both mother and son (George) are overcome by emotion when they meet in prison at last. Mrs Rouncewell and Mrs Bagnet persuade George to accept some legal help, preferably after asking Mr Jarndyce for advice. George, however, adamantly refuses to let his brother, the ironmaster, know about his plight.

Mrs Rouncewell then goes to the Dedlock town house where she tells Lady Dedlock about her son and the charge of murder brought against him. She implores Lady Dedlock's help and leaves a letter with her that she received while still at Chesney Wold.

When the old housekeeper has left, Lady Dedlock reads the letter. It is one more anonymous piece of writing accusing her of the murder of

Tulkinghorn. She is interrupted by Guppy's unexpected visit. Guppy, though he no longer wants to marry Esther, feels bound by his loyalty to her to tell Lady Dedlock that the letters he thought had been burnt at Krook's have actually not been destroyed. He proceeds to ask her about this morning's visitors (Mr Smallweed, Mr and Mrs Chadband and Mrs Snagsby) and warns her that these letters must have been used in order to extort money from her husband.

When he has left, Lady Dedlock has these visitors described by a footman. Feeling threatened by the anonymous letter-writer, and by dead Mr Tulkinghorn, she collapses, realising that her husband must now know about her secret.

She leaves the house secretly, abandoning all her possessions. In a letter to Sir Leicester she confesses her guilt, and tells him that she did actually go to Tulkinghorn's on that fateful evening, but that she is innocent of his death. She finally bids him to forget her.

Chapter 56: Pursuit

Some time later, Volumnia, bored and inquisitive, enters the library and rummages among Sir Leicester's papers. She stumbles over Sir Leicester himself, stretched out on the floor. The whole house is in a flurry now, but Lady Dedlock cannot be found anywhere. Her farewell letter is discovered on her table.

It takes some time before Sir Leicester, close to death, regains consciousness. The attack has left him an invalid, unable to speak coherently any more. Mrs Rouncewell looks after him. He is shown Lady Dedlock's letter and faints again. When he recovers, Bucket, who is already in the house, is summoned to him. Bucket reads Lady Dedlock's letter and he understands from Sir Leicester's desperate signs and incomplete messages scrawled on a slate that he is to trace Lady Dedlock, and to inform her that she is forgiven. He leaves at once, after reassuring Mrs Rouncewell that she need not worry about her son any more.

Darkness has fallen and Bucket starts his quest, beginning with Lady Dedlock's rooms; he finds a handkerchief marked 'Esther Summerson' and takes it with him. He then rushes by coach to George's shooting gallery, where he gets Esther's London address from George, who is back at his establishment again. Next he hurries to Mr Jarndyce, explains everything to him and tells him that he needs Esther with him in order to allay Lady Dedlock's suspicions, if he manages to find her.

While Esther gets ready, Bucket is trying to guess at Lady Dedlock's whereabouts. He includes the possibility of her committing suicide. He could not possibly think of the place where she discovered Esther's handkerchief: Jenny's hovel near the brick-kilns.

NOTES AND GLOSSARY:

Death and the Lady: a common Renaissance motif, a skeleton courting a lady

hammer-cloth: cloth covering the driver's seat

sticks of state: long staffs carried by footmen

models in a caravan: waxworks, carried in caravans, and exhibited at shows

Almack's: fashionable establishment where dances and other social functions were held

unbear him: loosen his (the horse's) harness

Chapter 57: Esther's Narrative

Esther sets off with Bucket. Answering his questions, she tells him that apart from her guardian she can't think of anyone but Mr Boythorn in whom her mother might confide. They leave a description of Lady Dedlock at a police station. They then stop at a ghastly place near the Thames; but the drowned body shown to Mr Bucket is not the one they feared to find.

The coach is now rattling away to St Albans, with Bucket asking everyone for further information. They are on Lady Dedlock's trail now, the inspector says. When arriving at Bleak House, Esther is told by Bucket that he watched her and Charley bring poor Jo to the house. He explains to her that he urged Jo to leave London for fear that he might become too talkative about Lady Dedlock.

Looking up at the room in Bleak House that Skimpole usually occupies, Bucket is able to show that he has seen through him. He tells Esther that Skimpole accepted a five-pound bribe from him so that Jo could be taken away on the very night he was so badly ill, and Esther considers this to be great treachery on Skimpole's part.

There is no clue to Lady Dedlock's whereabouts at Bleak House, so they move on to Jenny's house, because on their way to St Albans Esther has explained to Bucket how her mother got the handkerchief.

At the brickmaker's hovel they find Liz and the two sulky, silent husbands; Jenny is not in. Liz's husband threatens his wife not to talk too much. Jenny's husband reluctantly relates that a lady did come to their place the previous night, that she inquired about Esther, and that she had a brief rest before leaving with Jenny, who apparently went to London, whereas the lady chose the opposite direction. Bucket supposes that Lady Dedlock left her watch with the brickmakers, as Jenny's husband was more precise than usual about time. But why should she have done so?

Their carriage now moves north; it is snowing hard, and the cold and the slush make progress difficult. Bucket still goes on gathering information about a lady fitting his description. After a brief, but absolutely necessary rest, Bucket, whose information has grown scarce, says 'he has got it' and decides to move back to London as fast as possible. They are back upon the same road they have come and Bucket attempts to reassure Esther, who is now quite desperate, that he will stand by her, no less than by Sir Leicester.

NOTES AND GLOSSARY:

barouche: four-wheeled carriage with the driver's seat high in front

Woodpecker-tapping: from another song by Thomas Moore

fypunnote: five-pound note

Chapter 58: A Wintry Day and Night

We are back at the Dedlocks' house in London. Rumour is spreading fast now in the neighbourhood and among all Sir Leicester's acquaintances – whether tradesmen or politicians. Sir Leicester has had his bed brought to the window. Unable to speak distinctly, he has to write all his orders for Mrs Rouncewell on a slate. He orders a fine fire to be lit in Lady Dedlock's room. But Mrs Rouncewell tells George, who is keeping her company, about her fears that the step on the Ghost's Walk will walk her ladyship down, and about her apprehensions that the Dedlock family is disintegrating.

Volumnia Dedlock, bored at her brother's sick-bed, indiscreetly mentions George Rouncewell, whom Sir Leicester knew as a boy. Sir Leicester has him summoned to his room at once. His impaired powers of speech have a little improved through sheer excitement.

Sincere and warm greetings ensue, and Sir Leicester gallantly declares that his love for his wife has remained unaltered. After this strain he gets worse, with Mrs Rouncewell and her son faithfully looking after him until an ominous dawn is breaking.

NOTES AND GLOSSARY:

untaxed powder: snow; unlike the powder on the footman's hair, which was subject to tax

to auger: to predict; 'to auger' should possibly read 'to argue', which would make better sense

rustic boyhood: boyhood spent in the country

Chapter 59: Esther's Narrative

That same morning Esther and Bucket return to London. Esther still does not understand Bucket's motives for hurrying back, but she feels that he must have very good reason. Bucket directs their coach to what seems to Esther the most horrible streets in London. Here the inspector gets some valid information from various policemen on duty. They then proceed on foot to Chancery Lane. On their way they meet Allan Woodcourt. Allan has spent the night at Richard's abode, and says that Richard is deeply depressed. Esther fully appreciates his help. They have reached the Snagsbys' house and Bucket asks for Allan's medical help in getting a piece of paper from Guster, who is having fits and is unwilling to unclench her hand.

Mr Bucket blames Mrs Snagsby for having thrown her poor maid into such a fit, through her unreasonably jealous behaviour. Allan in the meantime has managed to get the paper from Guster. It is a letter written in portions, at different times, by Esther's mother. Lady Dedlock wrote the first words at Jenny's home. She then left the brickyard, convinced that she was going to die both of terror and exhaustion. She was (in the third part of the letter) looking for a place to die. Her last scribbled word is 'Forgive'.

Guster is now able to relate to Esther how a wretched woman stopped her outside the Snagsbys' house for directions to the burying-ground. She gave her that letter.

Allan, Bucket and Esther now go to that awful cemetery, Guster's words still ringing in Esther's ears. In front of the iron gate they find a woman lying on the ground. Esther thinks it is Jenny. But Bucket has guessed correctly: there were two women, they exchanged clothes, and one of them went back to London. Thus Esther finds her mother dead at the gate of the very cemetery where Captain Hawdon lies buried.

NOTES AND GLOSSARY:

the whole bileing: 'the whole boiling', a full lot of laundry, colloquial for 'the whole lot'

Chapter 60: Perspective (*Esther's narrative*)

After this shock Esther is ill for a short time and stays with her guardian in London. She is touched by the gentleness of all those around her. Mr Jarndyce tells her that Bleak House will have to look after itself for a while, that their presence in London is needed by Ada and Richard, who is still as hostile as ever toward Mr Jarndyce. But according to John Jarndyce, Richard is the victim of Chancery and he will soon see everything 'with clearer eyes' again.

During Esther's illness Mrs Woodcourt has come to Mr Jarndyce's house. He and Esther find her more agreeable than she used to be. There is now 'less pedigree' about her. She is going to stay so that her son can visit her more easily. Mr Jarndyce also informs Esther that Allan will not go abroad, but will probably be appointed medical attendant for the poor, somewhere in Yorkshire.

Esther visits Ada daily in her shabby lodgings. She notices that the young household grows poorer every day and that Vholes's activities swallow up whatever money Ada owned. One day she meets Miss Flite, who confirms her suspicions that Vholes is a dangerous person. As Richard is the most constant suitor in Court she has appointed him her executor; she has also added two new birds to her collection, which she calls 'the Wards in Jarndyce'.

That same evening Richard brings Vholes for dinner. Vholes manages to have a short, private talk with Esther, telling her that 'C is in a bad way' and stating his opinion that Mr C's marriage was very ill-advised. Vholes having left, Allan Woodcourt presently comes and takes Richard for a walk. Ada confides to Esther that she is truly worried about her husband, but that she hopes the child she is expecting may turn out to be a comfort to him – if Richard lives to see it.

Chapter 61: A Discovery (*Esther's narrative*)

Skimpole, his usual careless and superficial self, regularly visits the Carstones and Esther resents his sponging on Richard. She therefore decides to call on him, and after some hesitation asks him not to see Richard any more. Skimpole readily and shamelessly agrees; as he is not able to pay back the money he has borrowed from others, why should he 'give them pain?'

Before leaving Esther blames Skimpole for having betrayed Jo and consciously accepted a bribe from Bucket. Skimpole insists that he couldn't possibly be bribed, as money is of no value to him whatsoever. Quite playfully, in the manner of 'the house that Jack built', he proceeds to link all the events that made him accept that money.

Neither Esther nor her guardian ever again meets Skimpole, who dies a few years later, leaving behind him a diary in which he states that 'Jarndyce . . . is the Incarnation of Selfishness'.

Esther, faithful as ever, goes on paying her visits to Ada. Richard seems to dwindle away, comforted only by Allan Woodcourt's untiring loyalty. One night, while escorting her home, Allan declares his love to her. But Esther, both elated and saddened, has to tell him that her future is already 'bright and clear before her'.

NOTES AND GLOSSARY:

L, S, D: the standard abbreviations for pounds, shillings and pence (from the Latin, *librae, solidi, denarii*)

Chapter 62: Another Discovery (*Esther's narrative*)

Esther has gone to sleep with her guardian's letter, the contents of which she knows by heart, on her pillow. Next morning she is gently probing him about her still being a suitable mistress of Bleak House. They agree to marry the following month. At that moment Mr Bucket is announced.

Bucket has Grandpa Smallweed 'chaired' into the room. Smallweed has found a will, concerning Mr Jarndyce, among Krook's papers, but he is more than reluctant to produce that will. He finally does so, when he has been promised that he will be paid according to the value of the document.

Mr Jarndyce, together with Esther, immediately proceed to Kenge's offices. The will is valid and the age-old dispute can now be settled. Mr Jarndyce's interests are, however, considerably reduced, according to Kenge, though Ada's and Richard's are 'very materially advanced'. Vholes is sent for; he agrees that this is an important document, but remains quite calm otherwise. The chapter ends with Kenge praising the system of equity, his very words apparently cementing that system.

NOTES AND GLOSSARY:

chair that there Member: Old Smallweed is carried in a chair, like a
      successful candidate in a parliamentary election

Chapter 63: Steel and Iron

George has given up his shooting gallery. He stays at Chesney Wold attending on Sir Leicester, who is slowly recovering. He has, however, resolved to travel up north to the iron country to meet his brother. In the dark and grimy north, a 'Babel of iron sounds', he is struck by his brother's omnipresent renown. Amid the furnaces and the many people working for Rouncewell, George meets Watt, his nephew. Without disclosing his identity he is led to his brother's office by Watt, and gives his name as 'Mr Steel'. The ironmaster, however, recognises him almost at once. That very day Watt's engagement to Rosa is to be celebrated and George will, of course, be the most important guest. The following day Rosa is to go to Germany to improve her education.

Next morning, George, who is self-conscious about his past, confesses that he has come to ask some advice on how his mother is to be made to 'scratch' him (that is, leave him out of her will). Although appreciating the ironmaster's warm welcome and the offer of a job, George will not leave his mother or Sir Leicester's 'household brigade'. His brother agrees to look over and post a letter which George has written to Esther. Out of sheer delicacy he does not want to send it from Chesney Wold. In this letter George tells Esther that he is in possession of a sample of the handwriting of a 'certain person' (Captain Hawdon). It is a note asking him to deliver a letter to a beautiful lady. George also apologises for the fact that he had believed the captain dead and he ends by assuring Esther of his everlasting loyalty. As his brother does not object to posting that letter, George can take his leave, feeling at ease now.

NOTES AND GLOSSARY:

once and away: once in a while, occasionally

to bait: to rest when travelling

Chapter 64: Esther's Narrative

Esther has been given two hundred pounds by her guardian to spend on her wedding. Mrs Woodcourt is helpful, and Charley is busy with sewing. The marriage, as planned by Esther, will be a modest and quiet ceremony. Esther again nurtures some hopes concerning the outcome of Jarndyce and Jarndyce; her guardian, however, stays sceptical, and Richard is in a state of frenzied anxiety.

Mr Jarndyce has had to go to Yorkshire on business for Allan Woodcourt. Esther is astonished that Mr Jarndyce now wants her to join him there. He meets her at the hotel and informs her that he has looked for a suitable house for Allan and that he now wishes her help and her advice on how to equip it. Esther is of course deeply moved.

As they go to Allan's house next morning Esther finds that her guardian has meticulously arranged everything according to her own taste. She secretly hopes that Allan will not mind this. The house is to be called Bleak House.

Mr Jarndyce reveals to Esther how he became aware of her love for Allan, and how he came to consider his own affection as selfish. He regards himself as Esther's father now, as he gives her away to Allan.

They all return home next day. Esther accompanies her guardian to his house as she does not want to take her leave too abruptly. They are informed that Mr Guppy has already called three times. Esther has barely told her guardian about Guppy's former proposal when he is presently shown in, followed by his mother and Mr Weevle (Jobling). He is an attorney now, he owns a house and has discovered that Esther's image is still 'imprinted on his art', he therefore intends to be magnanimous and reiterates his proposal. This being refused, the three of them leave again, Mrs Guppy having become quite abusive and telling Mr Jarndyce to 'get out' of his own house in order to 'find someone good enough.'

NOTES AND GLOSSARY:

Fatima: Bluebeard's seventh wife, who wants to find out about the forbidden chamber (see also note to Chapter 53)

Chapter 65: Beginning the World (*Esther's narrative*)

The term has started and, filled with optimistic anticipation, Esther goes with Allan to Westminster Hall. On their way they meet Caddy in a hired carriage. As Caddy insists on telling Ada how much she owes Esther, they come to the Court rather late. The Court of Chancery is packed with such a crowd of people that they can neither see nor hear what is going on. They can hear only laughter. Asking for the reasons of this merriment Allan and Esther are informed by Kenge and Mr Vholes that the great cause is ended after so many years and that it must be paid for, in other words, the suit has swallowed up all of the estate in costs. Though quite shocked, Allan and Esther are however most apprehensive about Richard.

As Richard is still in Court Allan looks after him and takes him home. Later in the evening Esther and her guardian go to Symond's Inn as well. Richard, terribly weakened, is ready to start the world again, as he says. He is now fully conscious of his wrong behaviour and apologises to both Jarndyce and Ada. He then starts the world, though not this, our world.

After Richard's death, Miss Flite arrives, weeping, to tell Esther that she has set her birds free.

NOTES AND GLOSSARY:

the woolsack:	the seat of the Lord Chancellor in the House of Lords, here used to mean the Lord Chancellor himself
his silver trowel:	his silver tongue; Mr Kenge is a glib talker
Patience:	see Shakespeare's *Twelfth Night* (II.4.115–18)

Chapter 66: Down in Lincolnshire

Chesney Wold is a silent place now. Lady Dedlock's ashes have been brought to the family mausoleum and there is still some gossip, though subdued, about the 'profanation' of the Dedlocks' last resting-place.

Sir Leicester, invalid and almost blind, accompanied by George, can occasionally be seen riding through his woods and stopping at the mausoleum door. Although Boythorn and his neighbour, Sir Leicester, have suffered together 'in the fortunes of two sisters' the baronet does not know this and their old quarrel about a right of way still goes on, Boythorn knowing that he is keeping the old man in humour by so doing.

George now lives in one of the lodges of the park, and Phil Squod is busy about the stable-yards. Mr Bagnet and family are welcome guests.

Sir Leicester is still read to by Volumnia, though the other cousins keep away, except during the shooting season. Some rare public balls excepted, Chesney Wold has become a gloomy, depressing place throughout the year.

NOTES AND GLOSSARY:

nough t'sew fler up – frever: 'to sew a fellow up – for ever', enough to exhaust somebody completely

---

Chapter 67: The Close of Esther's Narrative

Esther has now been the mistress of the new Bleak House for seven years and she gives a last, retrospective report.

Ada's baby, a boy, was soon born after Richard's death, and is a true comfort to his mother. The two Bleak Houses are Ada's homes now, and Mr Jarndyce has insisted on becoming her and her son's guardian.

Esther has two little daughters. Charley is married to a local miller, and Emma, her younger sister, is Esther's new maid. Tom, her brother, is apprenticed to the miller.

Caddy has now a carriage of her own; she works very hard and is a brave person, with her husband lame and their little daughter deaf and dumb.

Mrs Jellyby has turned towards women's rights, which involves even more letter-writing.

Peepy is still under the patronage of old Mr Turveydrop and doing well in the Custom House.

A Growlery has been added to the new Bleak House, but the wind is never in the east these days. Though not rich, Esther and Allan thrive on their philanthropic work and Esther concludes on a note of sheer satisfaction.

Part 3

Commentary

Dating the events in the book

Bleak House (1853), together with *Hard Times* (1854) and *Little Dorrit* (1857), belongs to a set of novels in which Dickens develops those attacks against social and government institutions that he made on a more episodic level in his earlier works (compare the victim of Chancery in *Pickwick Papers* or the attacks on the Circumlocution Office in *Dombey and Son*).

As in previous novels, Dickens's earlier experience and training as a journalist, his gift for accurate description and his interest in pathetically ludicrous detail are noticeable again: Miss Flite, Gridley and Jo have had their models in real life, but the comic figures are now far less important than in his earlier works.

As so often Dickens laid the action of the book some years earlier, although the social problems and phenomena he was preoccupied with when writing *Bleak House* are present in the novel: the scandal of the Court of Chancery, sanitary reform and slum clearance, the detective branch of the Metropolitan Police Force, the philanthropists.*

It is difficult to situate this novel chronologically. Thus Esther quite deliberately omits the date of the letter sent to her by Kenge and Carboy (Chapter 3). As Humphrey House has pointed out in *The Dickens World*, the time references in *Bleak House*, though numerous, are occasionally contradictory. The Lord Chancellor of this novel may be a portrait of Lord Lyndhurst (in office 1827–30), whom Dickens watched as a young reporter. The railways erupting into Lincolnshire point to a later date. Inspector Bucket could not have hunted Lady Dedlock before 1844, when plain-clothes detectives were first appointed by Sir James Graham, then Home Secretary. On the other hand, both Mrs Pardiggle and Mr Turveydrop, an elderly man filled with a nostalgia for the Prince Regent, push the story back into the eighteen-thirties.

Esther writes the last section of her narrative (see the opening sentence of Chapter 67) when she has been 'full seven happy years . . . the mistress of Bleak House'. She might in fact have been writing at the date her creator wrote the novel (1852–3).

The events narrated in *Bleak House* could thus be placed in the early eighteen-forties.

*See Humphrey House, *The Dickens World*.

General background to the book

In Thomas Carlyle's *Past and Present* (1843) a poor Irish widow solicits help for her children and herself from various charitable establishments in Edinburgh after her husband has died. She is not helped by anyone:

> She sank down in typhus-fever; died, and infected her Lane with fever, so that 'seventeen other persons' died of fever there in consequence. The humane Physician asks thereupon, as with a heart too full for speaking, Would it not have been *economy* to help this poor Widow? She took typhus-fever, and killed seventeen of you! – Very curious. The forlorn Irish Widow applies to her fellow-creatures, as if saying, 'Behold I am sinking, bare of help: ye must help me! I am your sister, bone of your bone; one God made us: ye must help me!' They answer, 'No, impossible; thou art no sister of ours.' But she proves her sisterhood; her typhus-fever kills them: they actually were her brothers, though denying it! Had human creature ever to go lower for a proof?'*

In Charles Kingsley's *Alton Locke* (1850) typhus and other deadly diseases are brought from the tailors' sweat-shops with their disastrous working conditions to the homes of the rich.

In *Bleak House*, because of the tardy proceedings of Chancery (Chapter 16), whole estates decay, sheltering 'a swarm of misery', and from the poisoned sewage of Tom-all-Alone's disease and corruption, both figuratively and literally, flow upwards and reach the houses of the well-to-do, infecting or threatening all.

The message that Dickens distils from his social, humanitarian and political concerns, artistically shaped in the world of *Bleak House*, is clear:

> There is not an atom of Tom's slime, not a cubic inch of any pestilential gas in which he lives, not one obscenity or degradation about him, not an ignorance, not a wickedness, not a brutality of his committing, but shall work its retribution, through every order of society, up to the proudest of the proud, and to the highest of the high. Verily, what with tainting, plundering, and spoiling, Tom has his revenge.

(Chapter 46)

Furthermore, Dickens insists that on this vast social ladder (with the Lord Chancellor and the Dedlocks at the top and Jo at the very bottom) all influences move vertically up and down.

Just as the houses of Tom-all-Alone's crumble and men are made to live there like 'lower animals ... in an unintelligible mess' because of

*Past and Present, Everyman's Library, Dent, London, Book III, Chapter 2: p. 143.

Chancery, everybody else, from the shabby genteel to the aristocracy up in Lincolnshire, will be tainted as well. Harmless Miss Flite, whose talents to keep up 'some form of gentle appearance' must be admired, 'has felt something worse than the cold' and has recreated her own world of Chancery:

'I began to keep the little creatures,' she said, 'with an object that the wards will readily comprehend. With the intention of restoring them to liberty. When my judgment should be given. Ye-es! They die in prison, though. Their lives, poor silly things, are so short in comparison with Chancery proceedings, that, one by one, the whole collection has died over and over again. I doubt, do you know, whether one of these, though they are all young, will live to be free! Ve-ry mortifying, is it not?'

(Chapter 5)

Gridley has become 'the best joke they have in Chancery', Tom Jarndyce commits suicide, not without confessing that being a victim of Chancery is like 'being drowned by drops' (Chapter 5). Richard Carstone becomes maniacally obsessed by the suit and goes 'mad by grains', inheriting 'a legendary hatred' (Chapter 1). Miss Barbary and her sister Lady Dedlock are somehow linked to the case, probably 'without knowing how or why,' and, ironically enough, it is Lady Dedlock's former lover Captain Hawdon, alias Nemo, who earns a less than modest living by doing some legal copy-writing from the Jarndyce case for Mr Tulkinghorn through Snagsby.

Once we become aware of this dense social web with its numerous social and moral interdependences it is no longer astonishing that such an apparently haughty lady as Lady Dedlock should meet poor Jo, whose very name is so short that a shorter name couldn't be imagined, who is literally destitute of everything, without parents, surname, or relations, and with no education.

Dickens gives a comprehensive and complex view of society and because he insists on people being interdependent, his judgement is coherent as well. This is a moral universe and precisely because of the lack of moral and human concern Dickens is not only an imaginative master but also a radical judge of his age:

A band of music comes and plays. Jo listens to it. So does a dog – a drover's dog, waiting for his master outside a butcher's shop, and evidently thinking about those sheep he has had upon his mind for some hours, and is happily rid of. He seems perplexed respecting three or four; can't remember where he left them; looks up and down the street, as half expecting to see them astray; suddenly pricks up his ears and remembers all about it. A thoroughly vagabond dog, accustomed to low company and public-houses; a terrific dog to sheep; ready at a whistle to scamper over their backs, and tear out mouthfuls of their wool; but an educated, improved, developed dog, who has been taught his duties and knows how to discharge them. He and Jo listen to the music, probably with much the same amount of animal satisfaction; likewise, as to awakened association, aspiration or regret, melancholy or joyful reference to things beyond the senses, they are probably upon a par. But, otherwise, how far above the human listener is the brute!

Turn that dog's descendants wild, like Jo, and in a very few years they will so degenerate that they will lose even their bark – but not their bite.

(Chapter 16)

Jo, who stands for a whole class of similarly destitute people, is not, however, the only example. Dickens gives a compendious gallery of human types of every shape of human existence, and he leaves us wondering 'what has gone wrong?'

How is it possible that Captain Hawdon has grown so miserable that he literally gives up his identity (Nemo means 'nobody')? At his death he is covered by a handful of earth in a repulsive graveyard next to the dwellings of other poor people, in fact underneath a kitchen window (see end of Chapter 16).

Significantly enough there is not a single happy child in the story of *Bleak House*, and there are few decent parents (the only exceptions being the Bagnet family), but 'innumerable children have been born into the cause' (Chapter 1) and, like Miss Flite's birds, have grown up and died, withered by that same cause; similar to the birds, which certainly do not deserve pining away their short lives in a cage, 'scores of persons have deliriously found themselves made parties in Jarndyce and Jarndyce without knowing how or why' (Chapter 1).

As a child Esther sees in her godmother's face that it would have been far better if she had never been born (Chapter 3). Bruised, dirty and utterly neglected ('the dirtiest little unfortunates I ever saw', Chapter 4), the Jellyby children tumble about their ramshackle house. Mrs Pardiggle's five little boys are 'ferocious with discontent' (Chapter 8). Ada, still quite young, is grieved that she should be the enemy of a great many people without knowing why. Guster has come from one of the worst possible orphanages; Phil Squod, as a baby, was found in the gutter. Jenny's child dies in shockingly unhealthy surroundings. Neckett's children are abused, though it is certainly no fault of theirs that their father was a 'follower', and of Judith Smallweed we know that 'she never owned a doll, never heard of Cinderella . . . it is doubtful whether Judith knows how to laugh' (Chapter 21).

On the other hand, if Skimpole is a 'child', ('there is no one here but the finest creature of the earth – a child', Chapter 6), we soon notice that this sort of childhood – the selfish adult who never reaches maturity – is not very valuable, but the very reverse of 'fine'.

Chancery has soiled everything, and Dickens does not leave us in any doubt about it:

> This is the Court of Chancery; which has its decaying houses and its blighted lands in every shire; which has its worn-out lunatic in every madhouse, and its dead in every churchyard; which has its ruined suitor, with his slipshod heels and threadbare dress, borrowing and begging through the round of every man's acquaintance; which gives to monied might the means abundantly of wearying out the right; which so exhausts finances, patience, courage, hope; so overthrows the brain and breaks the heart; that there is not an honourable man among its practitioners who would not give – who does not often give – the warning, 'Suffer any wrong that can be done you, rather than come here!'
>
> (Chapter 1)

This is the central ganglion and from here the disease spreads and covers London, but it also reaches its suburbs and it extends to Lincolnshire and Shropshire. Like the fog, it covers all England, leaving everything indistinct, clammy and blurred as the waters that 'are out in Lincolnshire' and that make 'the oaken pulpits break out in a cold sweat' (Chapter 2). Everything is covered with a nasty, unhealthy film, which the reader wants to rip off or to peel away. Because everybody is touched and influenced by the same atmosphere, it follows that the same disease (Jo's) will infect all the classes and the same case (Jarndyce and Jarndyce) will influence and, with a very few exceptions, corrupt everybody in the novel.

No matter how savage Dickens's indictment is, there are no crudities in this novel. If institutions (whether the Court of Chancery or the Government) are outdated, complacent and parasitical and simply reflect human weaknesses, society is in a bad way. The Lord Chancellor behaves in a kindly way with Ada and Richard, but he is unable and unwilling to change the arrogance and parasitism that thrive around him. Sir Leicester is certainly a kind master, but he is complacently convinced of the supremacy of the party government of his times and 'he regards the Court of Chancery, even if it should involve an occasional delay of justice and a trifling amount of confusion, as a something, devised in conjunction with a variety of other somethings, by the perfection of human wisdom, for the eternal settlement (humanly speaking) of everything'. The reasons Dickens ironically advances for not altering anything are numerous: How could Mr Vholes possibly look after his aged father in the Vale of Taunton and his three daughters if he no longer had the possibility of sponging on his clients? The

Coodles, Doodles and Foodles as well as all the lawyers have their cognates in all the layers of society: how could the Smallweeds survive without their usury, the Chadbands without their religious, Skimpole without his artistic pretence? Old Turveydrop is a true tyrant, so are Mrs Jellyby and Mrs Pardiggle. Generally speaking, quite a few people 'have been insensibly tempted into a loose way of letting bad things alone to take their own bad course, and a loose belief that if the world go wrong, it was, in some off-hand manner, never meant to go right' (Chapter 1).

Dickens, however, insists that there is something wrong with a system that lets a poor human being, Jo, die of neglect and that allows other people (Snagsby, Nemo and Neckett) to depend on that same system in order to survive, however shabbily or modestly.

One chapter is appropriately titled 'Signs and Tokens', referring to the many documents that influence such a lot of people: Lady Dedlock gives away her secret when being shown an affidavit, Miss Flite always carries her documents about with her, Richard gives up a medical career in order to be able to study legal documents, Esther is summoned to London by a letter from Kenge's office that has to be read twice before any sense can be made of its abbreviations. The illiterate Krook lives among piles of documents, one of them being the will that brings the suit of Jarndyce and Jarndyce to its close. The man from Shropshire has to prove that he is his father's son. Tulkinghorn is more than eager to extort a piece of writing in Captain Hawdon's hand from George. Lady Dedlock (and the reader) are upset by anonymous bills. Mrs Jellyby and Caddy spend hours in futile letter-writing. Finally all these bags stuffed with paper lead to nothing else but a chillingly grotesque closing of the case: after Krook has disappeared among his rubbish, after Smallweed has exhausted himself and when Richard is agonising, those bundles and piles of documents are brought out of Westminster Hall with all the clerks laughing. It has all come to nothing, the estate is all used up in costs.

Why are so many people cryptographers, keen on deciphering documents or letters? They seem to have two different reasons. First we have people such as Esther and Richard who have to look for hidden pieces that they must fit together in order to find out the revealing pattern. Esther has to find out about the secrets surrounding her origin, Richard is compelled into discovering whether he is the rightful heir to the Jarndyce fortune.

Then we have Guppy, Mrs Snagsby, Old Smallweed, Hortense, Tulkinghorn and Bucket who are mainly interested in other people's secrets, so that they have power over them, that they can manipulate them or, in the case of Bucket, do their duty in a satisfying way.

Certainly *Bleak House* leaves some loose ends. Problems are not solved and no solutions are offered. We never come to know how the

Jarndyce and Jarndyce case originated or how large the estate or the sums involved may have been. But we do know that the law can be distorted, that people like Vholes can thrive whereas so many others die in complete destitution or oblivion.

In this brutal and diseased world, the unselfish characters are rare. Mrs Blinder, the Bagnets and Allan Woodcourt seem to be the most plausible ones in that group. It is more difficult to accept Esther's natural kindness or Mr Jarndyce's omnipresent, *deus-ex-machina** helpfulness but then, as in all Dickens's work, help comes, rather anarchistically, from the single individual, when Dickens the radical is at odds with Dickens the conformist.

The plot of *Bleak House*, just like melodrama and coincidence, belongs to fictional conventions that the modern reader may not always appreciate. As in *Little Dorrit* or *Our Mutual Friend* the plotting is inseparable from the social analysis and we do not discover any superfluous scenes or find any fault with the symbols in *Bleak House*. Because the symbols sustain the novel and reinforce the plot we readily accept the coincidences, resemblances and crossed lines of destiny. Thus Dickens could manipulate his characters within the world of *Bleak House* in order to give a complete kaleidoscope of the society he lived in at a point of crisis, and he could infuse into this novel his conviction that all men have an instinct for love and self-realisation which is again and again threatened by selfishness, irresponsibility and greed, all of them part of the human personality.

Structure and plot

Bleak House has two stories that run parallel and intermingle. These are the Jarndyce theme, wholly overshadowed by the corroding Chancery suit, and the Dedlock story. Esther, being Lady Dedlock's illegitimate daughter, and Tulkinghorn, Lady Dedlock's legal adviser who sees his suspicions about his client's past confirmed, bring the two strands of the narrative together. Esther is given thirty-three chapters out of a total of sixty-seven, though she has slightly more than half the novel at her disposal. Though Esther's autobiographical report moves as far back as her early years with Miss Barbary and also gives a brief account of her happy days at school in Reading, the two stories run parallel, covering a period of about four and a half years.

Esther, who finishes her narrative 'full seven years' after her marriage (Chapter 67) uses the past tense, the omniscient narrator uses the present tense. Hence the style of the two stories varies in intensity: Esther's

---

*Deus ex machina (*Latin*) means a god descending unexpectedly on stage from an elaborate piece of machinery, hence the meaning of 'sudden but improbable help'.

subdued and discreet character influences her narrative. Except for Chapters 57 and 59, in which she describes her mother's flight and her own as well as Bucket's anxious and harassing search for her, Esther has an impartial (she does not even give Allan Woodcourt the space he clearly deserves with her) but sensitive way of recording events, quite plausible for a person born outside the common social circle.

Born with a stigma, Esther accepts her lot in perhaps too docile a way and becomes a detached, but morally highly qualified observer of people around her. We might say that Dickens uses Esther as a brake on his exuberant imagination, though the unmistakable Dickens breaks through none the less in such descriptions as those of the Jellyby household and Krook's shop, or in the portrait of Skimpole, 'who has more the appearance of a damaged young man, than of a well preserved elderly one' or again in briefly introducing Mrs Guppy (Chapter 38).

Esther, unlike David Copperfield or Pip in *Great Expectations* (two more examples of first-person narrative), does not change at all and does not analyse her own growth towards maturity. She introduces herself with 'I am not clever. I always knew that' (Chapter 3) and she bids the reader farewell (Chapter 67), still confessing her astonishment that 'the people even like Me as I go about, and make so much of me that I am quite abashed.' Plain and submissive throughout the novel, she describes disasters as well as pleasant events with the same placidity. There is no special vocabulary linked to Esther, except for her diffident and almost reluctant way of giving her own impressions. We tend to forget her anonymous behaviour, however, because through her we look at an extraordinary multitude of characters, all presented in a visually very detailed way.

If Esther's viewpoint is necessarily narrow and simple, the omniscient and omnipresent narrator in the other chapters is able to encompass whole landscapes, as he swiftly moves from London to Lincolnshire and is furthermore able to scrutinise and concentrate on minor characters or details. Thus in the first chapter we move from Lincoln's Inn to the Essex marshes and the Kentish heights and back again to a 'foggy glory round his (the Lord Chancellor's) head' and to Mr Tangle's swallowing his own words ('Begludship's pardon'). As there is a continuous narrowing in of the scenes as presented by the omniscient narrator, who moves from a general view, though crammed with details, to an extraordinarily precise description of a character (Chapter 1, London and the world of Chancery; Chapter 2, Lincolnshire and the metropolitan world of fashion; Chapter 16, Tom-all-Alone's, are good examples of this technique), we welcome Esther's straightforward plodding way of relating events, which helps us to find our own way through the *Bleak House* maze. Furthermore, Esther being a static character, it is through her and her narrative that we are able to judge the development, change and occasional decay in others (Richard) or to situate them more firmly within the moral and social scale (Mrs Jellyby, Turveydrop, Skimpole).

Esther's story

Esther's early years at Miss Barbary's and at Reading are merely an introduction to that far more critical period in her life at Bleak House which brings the full revelation of her identity. During the years with John Jarndyce she is closely linked to Ada and Richard, both wards in Chancery, whose courtship and short married life she witnesses while at the same time recording the painful degradation of Richard's personality.

Though the modern reader can easily notice and remember the clues to her parentage, the effects of serialisation may have blurred these clues with the first readers of *Bleak House*. Such hints are given by Es+her herself, when she has 'a strange sensation of mournfulness' after visiting Nemo's room (Chapter 14) and, more obviously, when she associates 'something . . . with the lonely days at my godmother's' on first seeing Lady Dedlock at Chesney Wold (Chapter 18). Another, more direct clue is given by the narrator in Chapter 7, when Guppy is riveted by Lady Dedlock's portrait. Later, John Jarndyce (Chapter 17), when telling Esther all he knows about her origins and Miss Barbary's family, lists all the elements of knowledge so far available for the reader. We are told in the middle of the novel (Chapter 29) that Esther Summerson is Lady Dedlock's daughter. In Chapter 36, Lady Dedlock reveals her identity to Esther, who is recovering from her illness at Boythorn's house.

This revelation, and Tulkinghorn's behaviour as well, force Esther's mother to leave her home in a state of confusion, and thus the two main strands of the story are intertwined as Esther tries to follow her.

Sub-plots connected with Esther's story

The main sub-plot connected with Esther's story is the developing relationship between *Ada* and *Richard*, which we can follow to its very end, at Richard's death.

Several other subsidiary plots develop parallel to Esther's narrative. As Caddy Jellyby takes a blind trust in Esther, the reader can follow her story and that of her family. We are informed about Caddy's marriage to Prince Turveydrop, about her brother Peepy's being befriended by old Mr Turveydrop, and about her parents' fate. Caddy does well financially, although Dickens heaps misfortunes upon that young household: Caddy's husband can no longer work and her baby daughter is deaf and dumb.

Harold Skimpole's disastrous part becomes apparent only in Chapter 57, when Bucket relates to Esther that Skimpole accepted a bribe so that Jo could be found and made to leave Bleak House, though for Esther Skimpole has been a parasite from the very beginning.

Poor *Miss Flite* is regularly introduced into Esther's story. Her fate ominously anticipates and impressively illustrates Richard's ruin, as also does *Gridley's*.

Charley *Neckett* is saved from penury at her father's death by becoming Esther's maid. She later marries a miller in Yorkshire and her brother and sister, kept by kind *Mrs Blinder*, are also provided for.

Vholes, introduced to Richard by Skimpole, and at once correctly sized up by Esther, devours whatever is left of Ada's and Richard's fortunes, as for him 'the One Great Principle of English Law is to make business for itself'.

The Dedlock story

This second major theme opens with Chapter 2, and it is *Lady Dedlock* who is connected with Chancery and the Jarndyce suit. There are no other Dedlock ties with that case, though we are told (Chapter 18) that John Jarndyce met Lady Dedlock and her sister years ago (probably when Boythorn was still courting Miss Barbary).

Mr Tulkinghorn, the family's legal adviser, discovers by accident that a shabby law-writer was Lady Dedlock's former lover. His motives for undoing the Dedlock family and especially Lady Dedlock stay obscure. We do not know what prompted his hatred as well as his indiscretion, as he is known as a trustworthy repository of family secrets. We should notice, though, that Lady Dedlock's downfall is not entirely due to her being involved in the Jarndyce case, but to her earlier love-affair with Captain Hawdon.

Sub-plots mainly connected with the Dedlock story

Mrs Rouncewell, her two sons (*George* and *the Ironmaster*), her grandson (*Watt*) and his fiancée (*Rosa*) are all connected with Chesney Wold, but George is an important link between the two main strands of the story. As he gives fencing lessons to Richard, Esther comes to know him. When helping the dying Gridley and offering a last shelter to Jo, Esther again appreciates his generosity. As a good friend of Esther's father (Captain Hawdon) he is instrumental in delivering, though quite unwillingly, a piece of Hawdon's handwriting to Tulkinghorn. The story of the Bagnet family is subsidiary to George's story.

As *Mrs Snagsby* used to give some work to the law-writer, the Snagsby household is incidentally involved in the Dedlock theme.

Sub-plots connected with both themes

Guppy, deeply infatuated with Esther, finds out about her mother's relationship with Captain Hawdon, helped in his investigations by his friend Jobling.

Jo, the victim of neglect and disease, infects Esther, who convalesces at Boythorn's near Chesney Wold.

Krook, who owns the revealing letters, comes to know Esther. As he is *Mrs Smallweed's* brother his belongings go to that family and the Smallweeds are able to blackmail the Dedlocks.

Bucket comes late into the story; when he tries to find Lady Dedlock, he takes with him Esther, whom he previously met at George's shooting gallery.

Style

Dickens's powers of observation and description were unique. In *Bleak House* these talents help to stress the all-pervading feeling of helplessness of all those characters whose fate is directly influenced by the Jarndyce and Jarndyce suit.

Through the fog in the first chapter Dickens insists on the omnipresent influence and insidiously corrupting powers of Chancery. The results of this corruption will be illustrated by another perfectly homogeneous and coherent vocabulary in Chapter 16, in which he describes the slum of Tom-all-Alone's, itself the immediate result of tardy Chancery procedures. Similarly in Chapter 57 ('Esther's Narrative') the chilling atmosphere makes us anticipate Lady Dedlock's death.

Dickens also excels when giving detailed character descriptions and when situating these characters into their everyday surroundings. The ramshackle Jellyby house is echoed by the neglected children and by such details as Caddy's and Mrs Jellyby's clothes.

On the other hand Mr Jarndyce's house, although quaint and unusual from an architectural point of view, perfectly corresponds to its owner's peaceful and humane way of life. Richard Carstone's progressive physical and spiritual decay are paralleled by his successive dwelling-places. From his guardian's well-kept house he moves downwards through neglected barrack-rooms and finally dies in a hopeless state of near-poverty in Symond's Inn. Miss Flite's room is utterly bare, except for some birds, the names of which reflect those human aspirations that Chancery is seen to destroy. Nemo lives in a similar room, empty of nearly everything. 'Nothing' here equates with 'Nobody' (*nemo*).

Some of the characters are described twice: once, briefly but shrewdly, as first seen by Esther, and a second time, at greater length, when the narrator gives the reader a more comprehensive portrait. For example, re-read Esther's first meeting with Vholes:

> A sallow man with pinched lips that looked as if they were cold, a red eruption here and there upon his face, tall and thin, about fifty years of age, high-shouldered, and stooping. Dressed in black, black-gloved, and buttoned to the chin, there was nothing so remarkable in him as a lifeless manner, and a slow fixed way he had of looking at Richard (Chapter 37).

In Chapter 39 (which is also the opening chapter of the thirteenth of the nineteen monthly instalments of *Bleak House*) the omniscient narrator stresses his point once more: Symond's Inn is like 'a large dustbin of two compartments and a sifter', its materials 'took kindly to the dry rot and to dirt and all things decaying and dismal.' Mr Vholes's office blinks at 'a dead wall', the passage is 'dark', the door 'jet-black', there is a smell of 'unwholesome sheep', there is 'soot everywhere'. From these depressing surroundings we move to the man Vholes (a vole is a rat-like rodent), who, 'reserved and serious', with 'impaired digestion', 'is making hay of the grass which is flesh', for Vholes has discovered that the 'one great principle of English law is to make business for itself . . . . Viewed by this light it becomes a coherent scheme, and not the monstrous maze the laity are apt to think it.'

Surely Dickens means us to feel and to come to know that this *is* a maze, however, that his description of Vholes's office should be seen as a means of synecdoche, that is, a part standing for the whole and vice-versa. (Vholes stands for a whole body of lawyers, just as Jo stands for thousands of homeless poor.) Dickens sticks to this vocabulary and to the logics of his first argument: If we removed from Mr Vholes the 'grass which is human flesh' he would starve. 'Make man eating unlawful, and you starve the Vholeses!' (Chapter 34). Hence Vholes is no longer a simply unpleasant man; he becomes frankly sinister: 'Mr Vholes, quiet and unmoved, as a man of so much respectability ought to be, takes off his close black gloves as if he were skinning his hands, lifts off his tight hat as if he were scalping himself, and sits down at his desk' (Chapter 39). So it is only natural that, when Mr Vholes raps his desk, it should sound 'as hollow as a coffin'.

Later on (Esther writes) he occasionally gives a gasp 'which I believe was his smile.' This extraordinary example of imaginative coherence and richness is rounded off when Ada and Esther are informed that the estate has all been swallowed up in costs:

> . . . he gave one gasp as if he had swallowed the last morsel of his client, and his black buttoned-up unwholesome figure glided away to the low door at the end of the Hall.
>
> (Chapter 65)

Certainly Dickens exaggerates by giving an almost baroque wealth of detail (though this exaggeration can be part of his true indignation), but his imagination is perfectly controlled in *Bleak House*, leaving the impression of a genuine thematic complexity and depth. Whether it be Vholes, Tulkinghorn, Guppy or Phil Squod, or indeed any other character taken from this novel (with the exception of Ada and possibly Esther), it is nearly impossible to forget any of these figures and usually the clever choice of names adds to their unique nature.

If Dickens is sometimes carried away by his imagination in his previous novels (a 'weakness' that a majority of his readers seem to appreciate), he does not exaggerate or over-play the significance of symbolic detail in *Bleak House*. By repeating some symbols and metaphors he certainly adds to the unity of his novel. For example, the ever-pointing painted Roman can reveal his ominous symbolic meaning only at Mr Tulkinghorn's death. The Dedlocks' footmen, called 'Mercuries' from the very beginning, are later on changed into 'overblown sunflowers' (Chapter 48) and the reader readily accepts this further metaphor, as it only enhances the artificial and almost helpless status of these footmen.

Humour

Are there humorous episodes in *Bleak House*? If there are, then this humour is rather grating and we can smile only reluctantly when Dickens insists on the incongruous, almost surrealist aspect of a situation, thereby softening the impact of his criticism. Two examples can be considered here:

(i) when little Peepy Jellyby falls down some steps, Dickens points out the general neglect of these children on the one hand, but on the other hand cannot resist describing Richard's recording of the bumps of the child's head on the stairs (Chapter 4);

(ii) Phil Squod (Chapter 21) informs his master, George Rouncewell, that, as a baby, he was found not in a doorway, but in the 'gutter'. 'Watchman tumbled over me.' 'Then, vagabondizing came natural to you from the beginning,' replies George. As such, George's good-humoured quickness of repartee is funny, but because of this type of humour we tend to forget the truly horrible conditions in which so many children grew up.

Dickens's humour sometimes seems to be used as an instrument that enables him to take a more detached view of human weaknesses (see Chapter 21, 'The Smallweed Family'), of poverty and sheer destitution. George Orwell* suggests that 'Dickens may have had the sincerest

---

*George Orwell, 'Charles Dickens', in *Collected Essays*, Secker and Warburg, London, 1968, Vol. 1.

admiration for [simple people]. But it is questionable whether he really regards them as equal.'

Pathos

If Dickens's humour is part of his sympathy for his characters, so is his pathos, which the modern reader may not always appreciate. But *Bleak House* contains little that is maudlin; even the modern reader's compassion is aroused when Jo dies, and there is sincere indignation in the outburst at the end of Chapter 47: 'Dead, your Majesty. Dead, my lords and gentlemen. Dead, Right Reverends and Wrong Reverends of every order. Dead, men and women, born with Heavenly compassion in your hearts. And dying thus around us every day.'

Sir Leicester's physical decay and death are realistically and at the same time compassionately dealt with. The fact that Esther, in her more down-to-earth way, tells more than half of the story certainly helps to control emotions, and Esther gives an almost matter-of-fact report of her mother's death: 'I passed on to the gate, and stooped down. I lifted the heavy head, put the long dank hair aside, and turned the face. And it was my mother, cold and dead' (Chapter 59).

Names

The names Dickens chooses all fit his characters marvellously well. They can also betray perhaps in a slightly condescending way, something of the social origin of their bearers. Guppy, for instance, is a less imposing name than Tulkinghorn.

METAPHORICAL NAMES (in alphabetical order):

Badger: a grey-furred animal living in a burrow dug into the earth. The badger is said to be a shy and harmless animal

Bucket: this suggests various colloquial expressions and implies bustling cheerfulness

Clare: this suggests the verb 'to clarify', hence clear and free from impurities

Dedlock: a deadlock is a position in which it is impossible to act, a standstill

Flite: suggests both flight, running away from something, as well as 'to flit', to move about quickly and lightly

Guppy: gossipy

Jarndyce: old-fashioned pronunciation of 'jaundice', a disease caused by the stoppage of the flow of bile, marked by yellowness of the skin. A 'jaundiced' view is a view influenced by jealousy, envy or spite

Krook:	a crook is a person who makes a living by dishonest means;
Summerson:	the summer sun
Swills:	to swill is to wash by pouring a liquid through, or to drink greedily
Vholes:	a vole is a rat-like rodent
Volumnia:	from the late Latin *voluminosus*, occupying a lot of space

Barbary, Boythorn and **Smallweed** are further examples of openly metaphorical names that fit their owners well. Stylistically, these metaphorical names (including those whose meanings are elusive, such as **Jellyby** or **Tulkinghorn**) could not possibly be interchanged; they tend to classify and label their owners once and for all, sometimes unfairly. **Dedlock**, highly suggestive for the political and social influence of aristocracy, does not do justice to Sir Leicester, a chivalrous man. **Krook** seems to be more critical of the shop-keeper's nickname (Lord Chancellor) than of the man himself, who is, after all, a harmless eccentric.

Dickens was, of course, fully aware of the possible implications of names and of their appropriating power; hence the number of aliases in *Bleak House* is very revealing. Captain Hawdon, opting out of society, takes the alias of **Nemo**; young Smallweed, according to the author himself is 'metaphorically called **Small** and eke **Chick weed**, as it were jocularly to express a fledgling' (Chapter 20). Tony Jobling calls himself Mr **Weevle** (a weevil is a small beetle, which infests seed-stores). Jo is called **Toughy**, which is pathetically misleading.

Coincidence

Coincidence in *Bleak House* is less annoying and obtrusive than in earlier novels. This is due to the density of the language and the recurrence of the main symbols that cover or influence all the characters in the novel and make coincidence less artificial. Nevertheless some coincidences are troublesome.

The part played by Esther's handkerchief, which she leaves on the face of Jenny's dead baby, and which Lady Dedlock retrieves, and which Bucket uses as well, is very important, though well hidden.

Mr Boythorn is the Dedlocks' neighbour. Mrs Smallweed is Krook's sister. Miss Rachael marries Mr Chadband. Nemo was Trooper George's friend. Guppy visits Chesney Wold and sees Lady Dedlock's portrait. Esther meets Allan Woodcourt at Deal.

Dickens does not make much, however, of Esther's visit to Miss Flite (in the very house in which her father lies dying).

Characterisation

Esther Summerson

Esther introduces herself with the following words. 'I know I am not clever. I always knew that.... I would strive as I grew up to be industrious, contented, and kind-hearted and do some good to some one ... I hope it is not self-indulgent to shed these tears as I think of it ...' (Chapter 3). Later on, at Mr Jarndyce's, she confesses that she is 'a methodical, old-maidish sort of foolish little person' (Chapter 8).

This submissiveness and modesty may be resented by some readers, though we may argue that they are, at least for the first chapters of Esther's narrative, very much in keeping with the psychology of an illegitimate or unloved child. If her shrewd insights and her highly critical spirit may be astonishing at an early stage (with the Jellybys, for instance), we should be aware that in such passages the author's own indignation is more powerful than that of his heroine. Of course the humble portrait she gives of herself and the behaviour and comments we expect from such a person clash with the ironic, sharply discriminating assessment of those people she is going to meet. But Esther ought to be exonerated: together with John Jarndyce, Allan Woodcourt, George, Mrs Blinder and the Bagnets she belongs to those people whose very existence proves the healing power of compassion, generosity and private acts of charity. Furthermore her observation and (not self-acknowledged) intelligence do not make her the victim of such people of 'rapacious benevolence' whom John Jarndyce does not so easily see through.

When critically describing others, Esther has to face the dilemma of any honest narrator. She is reluctant to report, but her honesty requires her to do so, she is torn between an impulse to judge and the fear of being judged herself. She records what goes on around her sensitively, and such people as Mrs Jellyby or Mrs Pardiggle, but above all Skimpole and Vholes, are justly placed in the scale of values.

This technique and this indignation are, of course, more Dickens's own than his heroine's; through Esther the omniscient (and highly critical) narrator is reporting, and we tend to forget her, so fascinated are we by, for instance, the description of the Jellyby household, although it could be argued that Esther's being a social outsider and her alienation (caused by her early education) favour this critical vision and make it all the more plausible.

Technically she plays a major role: she brings together the two strands of the very dense fabric of this novel. As her memoirs occupy slightly more than half the book her presence and her personality help to give unity to the texture of *Bleak House*.

Her ways of describing people vary. She condemns Miss Barbary by praising her excessively. Skimpole is shown not only as a superficial person, but as a brutally insensitive man, as she subtly paraphrases him when he visits her at Boythorn's after her illness. On other occasions her critical judgement arises out of anxiety for someone she loves, as when she informs the reader that Richard had a carelessness which he mistook for prudence, or when she mainly dwells on the things that surround people and that tend to mirror their characters (the Jellyby lodgings or Mr Turveydrop's rooms). She can also manage to suppress a too biting form of irony: thus Mrs Woodcourt comes off rather well despite her painful insinuations.

Because Esther is modest her virtues and her feelings must be suppressed and Dickens's treatment of her personality is perfectly consistent. Being a demure person only her gratefulness may show. Hence she barely speaks to Allan Woodcourt, but she nearly marries John Jarndyce out of sheer respect and gratitude. This obedience goes so far that she does not object to her own name's being quite lost among the multitude of nursery rhyme and legendary names given to her by her tutor. She cannot escape the power of these nicknames and is almost completely appropriated by Mr Jarndyce. The fact that he has a new Bleak House built for her without her knowing anything about it is revealing.

As often with Dickens's main female characters, the physical outline is not precise at all. Like his illustrator, 'Phiz', Dickens used a stereotype for his heroines. Whereas the host of minor characters are sharply defined (how easy it is to imagine Mrs Bagnet or Mrs Guppy!) our image of Esther stays blurred.

Ada Clare

Ada, with 'her golden hair, soft blue eyes and such a bright, innocent, trusting face', is about seventeen years old when Esther meets her. She is shown as a loving, submissive and apprehensive girl throughout the novel. She is Esther's 'darling', and readily complies with Mr Jarndyce's suggestions without even giving a dynamic proof of her gratefulness. She is fully aware that merely by being born she has become the enemy of a number of people and that being involved in the Chancery suit means 'to be in constant doubt and trouble' all her life (Chapter 5). She loyally abides with Richard and readily gives him all her capital. The only independent step she makes is her secret marriage to Richard, which casts a 'shadow' on her relationship with Esther.

She stays very much the same after Richard's death, and modern readers may find her too passive or too good to be true.

Richard Carstone

Richard, a 'handsome youth, with an ingenuous face', is 'talking gaily, like a light-hearted boy' (Chapter 3) when Esther first meets him and Ada at the Lord Chancellor's.

His gay, good-humoured behaviour helps the two girls to overcome their shock when staying with the Jellybys. Miss Flite's experiences and especially Krook's telling them about the death of Tom Jarndyce (Ada's and Richard's grandfather), should at least make Richard sceptical of the outcome of the suit. He certainly resents, from the very start, John Jarndyce's well-intentioned and sound fatherly advice – not to lend any more money to Skimpole (Chapter 6) and above all not to court Ada any more if he expects to wrest any real success 'from Fortune by fits and starts' (Chapter 13).

Very soon Richard gives up the study of medicine, which he embarked on with artificial enthusiasm, and becomes an articled clerk at Mr Kenge's office. He is now able, as he puts it, to have his eye on 'the forbidden ground' (Chapter 17), but his involvement with the law accelerates his decline. He very soon tires of the law (Chapter 23) and tries the army, having incurred some debts in the meantime. As Mr Jarndyce talks sharply to him this time, warning him not to found a hope of expectation on 'the family curse' and asking him to relinquish any tie with Ada but his relationship (in other words, to give her up), Richard turns away from his guardian.

He now needs 'an embodied antagonist and oppressor' (Chapter 39), and finds him in Mr Jarndyce. His obsessive mania makes us foresee his fate even more clearly. Like Gridley, 'the man from Shropshire', Richard is haunted by Chancery. Although Dickens criticises his school education, which is certainly quite different from, say, that of Watt Rouncewell, Richard is above all the victim of his own instability and his fatal tendency 'to take his own carelessness for prudence', as Esther is quick to realise.

Accepting Skimpole as his best friend and relying on Vholes, who 'drives him away at speed to Jarndyce and Jarndyce', he soon 'looks the portrait of Young Despair' (Chapter 39; see also the illustration by 'Phiz'). Completely obsessed by the suit, 'the one subject that is resolving his existence into itself', he degenerates pitifully, secretly marrying Ada and using up all her capital. Wavering between extremes, his fits of hopefulness become even more painful than his bouts of despondency.

When the suit has come to its end and the estate has all disappeared in costs, Richard comes back to moral sanity.

John Jarndyce

Esther first meets her guardian and benefactor, a gentleman 'who looked very large in a quantity of wrappings', in the coach that takes her to the Reading boarding-school (Chapter 3). As he knows what happened to Tom Jarndyce, Mr John Jarndyce has withdrawn from all the legal entanglements of the case and tries to use his money benevolently and philanthropically on a number of causes.

He warns Richard not to trust too blindly in the outcome of the case and he advises him 'Trust in nothing but Providence and your own efforts' (Chapter 13).

Mr Jarndyce will not have anything more to do with 'Wiglomeration' (Chapter 8), the label he fixes to the multitude of documentation and seemingly endless and useless words spoken in the Court of Chancery. However, it takes him much longer than Esther, through whose eyes we mainly see him, to notice that he has misdirected his kindness and his money by helping the Sisterhood of Medieval Marys and the like (Chapter 8); we might even say that he is rather childish, if not obtuse, in his trust of Skimpole, whose meanness he is very slow to discover. When feeling ill at ease he becomes peevish and withdraws into his 'Growlery'; the wind, then, is 'in the East'.

As he is a Jarndyce himself and as his considerable private fortune must have come by inheritance, we cannot but wonder how it is that the Jarndyce inheritance does not influence him for the bad. John Jarndyce's advice and money, however, are of very little help with Richard, the Jellybys or the Pardiggles.

John Jarndyce, a non-such, seems to have all the virtues. It is, in fact, hard to imagine his having ever been really involved in such a corrupting law-suit.

A fatherly, almost a godly figure, his influence is considerable throughout the novel. Once he has released Esther, he takes Ada with him. The old Bleak House being empty, he builds a new one in Yorkshire (to which the young Woodcourt household adds a 'Growlery').

We can understand that Esther's gratitude towards him is boundless, but the facts that she 'feels towards him as if he were a superior being' and that she is close to giving up her hopes of Allan Woodcourt make us feel slightly uneasy. Does John Jarndyce really release Esther? The old nicknames are still there, 'just the same as ever' (Chapter 67), Bleak House is rebuilt in the North, Mr Jarndyce is known by no other name than that of 'guardian' to Ada's son and Esther's children. Therefore Esther's 'just the same as ever', which may have suggested absolute paradisiac domestic bliss to Dickens's readers, leaves us more sceptical today. Is all this kindness and self-abnegation not a subtle means of appropriating another person?

Lady Dedlock

Lady Dedlock is shown as 'bored to death' in Chapter 2, the opening lines of which link a whole class, ('a deadened world, and its growth is sometimes unhealthy for want of air') to rain-sodden Lincolnshire where 'there is a general smell and taste as of the ancient Dedlocks in their graves'.

'Her part in [the Jarndyce and Jarndyce suit] was the only property my Lady brought' her husband; 'a whisper goes about that she had not even family' and that Sir Leicester 'married her for love'.

Lady Dedlock, however, keeps her station in society quite well. Impassive, haughty and aloof, nothing seems to be able to disturb her: 'How Alexander wept when he had no more worlds to conquer, everybody knows – or has some reason to know by this time, the matter having been rather frequently mentioned. My Lady Dedlock, having conquered her world, fell, not into the melting, but rather into the freezing mood' (Chapter 2).

The illustrations by 'Phiz' add to this impression. Readers would certainly not suspect this lady, whose portrait can be found in the Galaxy Gallery of British Beauty (Chapter 20) to be Esther's mother, if it were not for Mr Guppy who discovers a likeness.

She does give herself away, though, first to Tulkinghorn when being shown the affidavit in her former lover's hand (Chapter 2) and a second time to Esther (and the reader) when 'those handsome proud eyes seemed to spring out of their languor, and to hold mine' (Chapter 18).

By eliciting John Jarndyce's only ironical sentence, apart from his dealing with Mrs Guppy, we are made aware of Lady Dedlock's past, which must have been very different from her present aristocratic ways ('you have achieved so much, Lady Dedlock'; Chapter 18). But in Chapter 36, when Lady Dedlock knows that her daughter is alive and when she has a meeting with her which is cruelly honest in its outspokenness (though perhaps distasteful to the modern reader), she concedes that she is travelling 'a dark road', that her apparent haughtiness is nothing but 'self-protection'.

From now on she is torn between two loyalties, and she eventually chooses deadly escape from both. At her death we become suddenly aware that this boredom on which Dickens insists so much was by no means some form of aristocratic arrogance, but a desperate attempt to hide a perpetual concentration on her own past. The more Lady Dedlock attempts to suppress her love for Captain Hawdon and her thoughts about her daughter, the more irresistibly and swiftly does she have to acknowledge the pressures and influence of her past and to reaffirm her true self.

She is thus the best example of one theme Dickens certainly

introduces into this novel: the constant though quiet suffering of people successfully hiding a tormented inner life (such as Tulkinghorn, George, Nemo and even Esther herself).

Sir Leicester Dedlock

Dickens gives a meticulous portrait of the baronet in Chapter 2: 'an honourable, obstinate, truthful, high-spirited, intensely prejudiced, perfectly unreasonable man'. In Chapter 18 he emphasises the difference in age between Sir Leicester and his wife.

If Dickens's portrait of the aristocracy in *Bleak House* is consistent from the political and social point of view (he shows the Dedlocks as politically retrograde, in resorting to bribing the electorate, and as socially naïve, when likening Mrs Rouncewell's son to Wat Tyler), he nevertheless gives some moral credit to the Dedlocks: Sir Leicester is obviously a fine master who gets on very well with his staff, especially with Mrs Rouncewell. It is revealing that George stays with the invalid baronet and rejects his brother's offer to start a career in the industrial north. Dickens's ambiguous attitude towards the British aristocracy seems to be fully reflected in this portrait. On the one hand we are sarcastically informed that Sir Leicester 'would on the whole admit Nature to be a good idea (a little low, perhaps, when not enclosed with a park-fence), but an idea dependent for its execution on your great country families' (Chapter 2); on the other hand Dickens appreciates the landscaping around Chesney Wold and the building itself (Chapter 36). If there is no 'superabundant life of the imagination' (Chapter 7) with Sir Leicester, his 'gallantry to my Lady, which has never changed since he courted her, is the one little touch of romantic fancy in him' (Chapter 2).

We, the readers, know that the baronet's gallantry will never cease, and although his cousins are seen as caricatures, leading pompous and useless lives, Sir Leicester comes out as a genuinely good man. His unwavering gallantry is truly moving, and there is a note of regret in Chapter 66: 'passion and pride . . . have died away from the place in Lincolnshire, and yielded it to dull repose.'

Mr Tulkinghorn

Mr Tulkinghorn is 'of what is called the old school' (Chapter 2). As a solicitor to the Court of Chancery and as the Dedlocks' legal adviser, he is 'a retainer of family secrets'. His demeanour, his clothes, all express 'the steward of the legal mysteries, the butler of the legal cellars of the Dedlocks'. His deferential behaviour is misleading and under his gaze Lady Dedlock is certainly not the 'inscrutable Being' she thinks she is.

In fact Mr Tulkinghorn, 'this oyster of the old school, whom no one can open', enjoys the power his secret knowledge gives him over supposedly important people. It is he, like the fashionable jewellers and mercers in Chapter 2, who manipulates his employers; he understands their affairs (Lady Dedlock does not know where she stands in the Jarndyce and Jarndyce suit) and it is this gratification of his desire for power which is his main stimulus, though it will also destroy him. Because Tulkinghorn despises people, he eventually goes too far and 'the ridiculous Roman' then takes on another, more sombre meaning.

Tulkinghorn enjoys hurting his clients. Thus he clearly relishes telling Sir Leicester that Rouncewell has beaten him in the elections; he enjoys informing Lady Dedlock by an insolent piece of fiction that he has discovered her secret: 'I leave you to imagine, Sir Leicester, the husband's grief' (Chapter 40). He coarsely exploits Hortense, who murders him.

Nevertheless, we can pity this man, who, when alone and trying to enjoy his priceless port, tends to think of 'that one bachelor friend of his, a man of the same mould and a lawyer too, who lived the same kind of life until he was seventy-five years old, and then, suddenly conceiving (as it is supposed) an impression that it was too monotonous, gave his gold watch to his hairdresser one summer evening, and walked leisurely home to the Temple and hanged himself' (Chapter 22).

Allan Woodcourt

The 'dark young surgeon' who is present at Nemo's deathbed, and who knew Nemo (Esther's father) when he was alive, has cast a discreet but powerful spell on Esther. Whatever he does, he is personally much concerned. Nemo's addiction to opium is of professional interest to him, but he also notices that there was something in the poor law-writer's manner 'that denoted a fall in life' (Chapter 11). His warm humanity and his kindness bring him into contact with many human 'shipwrecks', and his being a ship's surgeon for a while is highly symbolical. Like most of Dickens's good characters he is no theorist, but he believes in direct personal help to assist the needy. This attitude brings him to Tom-all-Alone's and to the shooting gallery; it also makes him visit Richard regularly and take up a materially unrewarding job in Yorkshire.

Guppy

Parallel to Tulkinghorn, Guppy patiently makes his own investigations into Lady Dedlock's secret and Esther's origin. His motives are quite honourable and he merely wants to attract Esther's attention, as he became infatuated with her when taking her, first to Kenge and Carboy's, and then to the Jellybys'.

Guppy is clumsy, in speech as well as in action. His use of legal terminology when withdrawing his marriage proposal is both pathetic and ludicrous. His last visit to Lady Dedlock turns out to be fatal: though he has been very loyal so far, and has not divulged her secret, Guppy now feels compelled to warn Lady Dedlock that old Smallweed means mischief with Captain Hawdon's letters which he discovered at Krook's. Lady Dedlock does not wait to be forgiven, but rushes out towards her death.

Guppy is an honourable young man (he does not want any money for Hawdon's letters; see Chapter 29), he is extraordinarily chivalrous, he does not desert his vulgar and waggish mother. Guppy finds it difficult to climb the social scale, but he eventually sets up his own practice as a lawyer. Though his social origins are similar, his character is quite the opposite of that of Uriah Heep in *David Copperfield*.

Mrs Jellyby and Mrs Pardiggle

The breed of the Mrs Jellybys will probably exist in any age. She is the perfect illustration of misguided humanitarianism. Spending vast amounts of energy and money on the impossible scheme of sending English settlers to Central Africa, she thoroughly neglects her own family and seems to have become utterly unconscious of the misery in the slums close at hand.

Similarly Mrs Pardiggle, in whom one may see a 'Puseyite', smugly informs Esther that she takes her children with her everywhere; but she only manages to make them desperately unhappy. She takes pride in the fact that she is able to carry on her work in a stubborn way, though she has no success at all. Whatever she does, she can, at very best, offer only a varnish; to quote Carlyle, she tries to 'cure a world's woes by rose-water'.

Jenny's brutish husband sees the true problems in a much more realistic way than Mrs Pardiggle:

'Is my daughter a-washin? Yes, she is a-washin. Look at the water. Smell it! That's wot we drinks. How do you like it, and what do you think of gin, instead! An't my place dirty? Yes, it is dirty – it's nat'rally dirty, and it's nat'rally onwholesome; and we've had five dirty and onwholesome children, as is all dead infants, and so much the better for them, and for us besides. Have I read the little book wot you left? No, I an't read the little book wot you left.'

(Chapter 8)

Part 4

Hints for study

NOTES SUCH AS THESE may help you to study and to understand *Bleak House* better. If you can manage to read some of the texts suggested in Part 5, all the better. But no amount of critical writing, no matter how excellent, can be a substitute for a close reading of the novel.

There are so many characters in *Bleak House* that you may easily forget the functions of some of them.

In order to remember even minor characters, you should try to concentrate on one of the two plots: Which are the persons mainly connected with the Dedlock family? Which are those linked to the Jarndyce case? Who is instrumental in making the lines of the narratives cross?

Answering examination questions

Questions on characters

In answering examination questions on a particular character, stick to the information *the author* gives you. What do we know about him or her? How do we receive this information? Do we see a character through Esther's eyes, or is it Dickens himself who is introducing him or her to us? The way these people live, the language they use, the way they deal with other characters, tell us a great deal about them.

For example, you might reconsider Tulkinghorn. Find again those chapters in which he appears. Read those passages which concern him very carefully. Take, for instance, those three short passages in Chapter 16 ('In his chambers, Mr Tulkinghorn sits meditating . . .'). How much does Dickens, almost casually, tell us here about the relationship between Tulkinghorn and Lady Dedlock?

Or take Sir Leicester. How is our opinion of him formed? Have a good look at the portrait Dickens gives of the baronet in Chapter 2. But how does Esther see him in Chapters 18 and 43? Think of his relationship to his cousin. Notice his behaviour towards his servants. Does his gallantry towards his wife surprise you? When do we start having a more definite opinion of the baronet? Ask yourself which character has stayed most vividly in your mind and why? Dickens excelled in creating popular characters that are sometimes much better remembered than the theme of the book (for example, Mrs Gamp in *Martin Chuzzlewit*).

Questions on theme and story

You should read and analyse the following chapters very carefully: 1 ('In Chancery'), 16 ('Tom-all-Alone's'), and 40 ('National and Domestic'). Each of them provides a central element meant to symbolise one scandalous aspect of the society Dickens is attacking.

Esther's own quest for identity is crucial in the novel and easily remembered. You can re-read Esther's narrative and at the same time discover more about the sub-plots. Always remember to consider how each story is related to Esther's own. When does she come to know Richard? What does she think of him? When does John Jarndyce first tell her about the misgivings he has concerning Richard?

It can be both amusing and useful to re-read those chapters again in which Inspector Bucket appears and to see how many conventions of the detective story Dickens is using (you should bear in mind that the detective story was a new genre at that time).

Try to answer the following questions for yourself. If you feel strongly about a character (you may, for instance, not like Richard), you should not hesitate to write down your own opinion, but always give the corroborating quotation or passage from the text.

Some sample questions, and hints on answering them

(1) Explain the title of *Bleak House*.

'Bleak House' was not the first name of the Jarndyce home (see Chapter 8). When and why was its name changed into the more appropriate 'Bleak House'?

(2) How are the different characters affected by the Jarndyce suit?

Go through the list of characters. How much are these people involved? How do they react to the outcome of the suit?

(3) What is 'Wiglomeration'?

Re-read Chapter 8 and write down in your own words what the word means to Mr Jarndyce.

(4) What was Esther's early life like?

Esther sums up her first eighteen years in the first chapter of her narrative (Chapter 3). How much are we told about Miss Barbary and Mrs Rachael? What does Esther think of these two women (see the notes on Esther)? What was life like at Greenleaf? Mention Esther's state of mind at her godmother's, at Reading. Notice that she twice deliberately omits all precise dates of reference.

---

(5) How does Esther see the Jellyby household?

The street in which the Jellybys live reminds Esther of an 'oblong cistern to hold the fog'. There is first a general impression of confusion. One child has got its head caught in the area railings, and another one tumbles unattended down a whole flight of stairs. The second impression is one of complete neglect. What is the general appearance of these children? Carefully analyse the vocabulary Dickens uses when describing the servant-girl, Mrs Jellyby and Caddy. Mention some details in the description of this household that strike you as particularly incongruous.

---

(6) Write brief notes on the characters of the following: Esther, John Jarndyce, Ada, Richard, Sir Leicester and Lady Dedlock.

Make your own assessment, using the book itself and referring to the notes on 'Characterisation', p. 89.

---

(7) Give a detailed analysis of Mr Bucket's character.

We first meet Inspector Bucket in Tulkinghorn's room (Chapter 22), then at Gridley's death-bed in the shooting gallery (Chapter 24). He cunningly wins George's confidence (Chapter 49) and then arrests him for the murder of Tulkinghorn. Chapters 53–7, as well as Chapters 59 and 62, show Inspector Bucket as an efficient detective, who is conscious of the importance of his task. Give examples of Bucket's professional accuracy, show how his job forces him to take unpopular measures. Is Bucket a mere sleuth? What compliment does he pay Esther? Is he able to detect motives?

---

(8) Are there any truly successful people in *Bleak House*?

Only the actively good people are eventually able to lead decent lives and follow a not necessarily financially rewarding job (Allan and Esther). Neckett's children seem to do modestly well. Caddy is materially well off, though she has to cope with other hardships. The vast majority of the many characters in *Bleak House* do not achieve what they had intended. Richard does not become a wealthy man; in fact on his death he leaves Ada a poorer person than she was before. John Jarndyce does not marry Esther, nor can he save Richard from misery. Lady Dedlock cannot spare Esther. Sir Leicester's world is ruined. Tulkinghorn is a quietly unhappy man (see 'Characterisation', p. 94). Old Smallweed does not win a fortune by blackmailing the Dedlocks. Krook dies before he is able to elicit any meaning from the documents he owns.

---

(9) How are children shown in *Bleak House*?

What is Esther told as a child at one of her birthdays (Chapter 3)? Show what happens to the Jellybys' or the Pardiggles' children (Chapters 4 and 8). Think of the brickmaker's children (Chapter 8), of Jo and Guster (Chapter 15). Do not forget Skimpole's daughters and the young Smallweeds.

---

(10) How do their surroundings reflect the behaviour and manners of some of the characters?

See 'Vholes' in the notes on 'Style', p. 85. Compare the state of the Jellyby house with the situation of that family. How do the Smallweeds' lodgings echo their miserliness (Chapter 21)?

---

(11) Who are, apart from Esther, the truly generous characters in the novel?

Give examples of the generosity and kindheartedness of Allan Woodcourt, George Rouncewell, Jenny and Guster.

---

(12) What does Dickens think of aristocratic party government?

See Chapter 40. Is there any direct relationship between representative and represented? Carefully read the opening paragraphs of this chapter. What do these comic (and interchangeable) names suggest?

---

(13) In which chapters is Dickens's social and political criticism at its most powerful?

Chapters 1, 16 and 40; these deal with Chancery procedures, slums and political parties respectively.

---

(14) How important is Krook?

Explain his nickname (the 'Lord Chancellor'). Krook, although an illiterate man, knows all the names of the families involved in the suit (Chapter 5). He is able to give hints of what will happen to Richard. What is the symbolic meaning of his death? (See note to Chapter 32.)

(15) Choose one incident or description from *Bleak House* that you find amusing.

Although Dickens's humour is of the grim kind in this novel, some scenes are frankly funny. Choose among the following chapters the scene you can discuss best and suggest why you think it is amusing: 20 (Guppy and his friends at the eating-house), 27, 49 (the Bagnets' home, Mrs Bagnet's birthday-party), 11, 33 (the inquests held at the Sol's Arms).

(16) What are the reasons put forward by some of the characters for *not* abolishing Chancery?

What does Sir Leicester think of the Court of Chancery (Chapter 2)? How does Dickens see Vholes's fate if English law were changed (Chapter 39)? What does Conversation Kenge say about equity (Chapter 62)?

(17) Contrast the reasons given by the characters of the question above with John Jarndyce's opinion, Ada's feelings, Miss Flite's reactions or Dickens's views?

For Ada and Miss Flite, see Chapter 5, for John Jarndyce, Chapter 8, for Dickens, Chapter 1.

(18) What is the cause of Lady Dedlock's ruin?

Because she is one of the claimants in the Jarndyce case, Lady Dedlock is shown some affidavits written by her former lover, Captain Hawdon. More important, though, are Guppy's discoveries, the letters left by Hawdon, and the fact that her daughter did not die at birth as her sister told her.

(19) Do you consider Lady Dedlock's fall (for the reasons mentioned above) a defect of the plot?

As Dickens's plan – that the Jarndyce lawsuit taints everybody who touches it – is logical and complete, you may consider the reasons for Lady Dedlock's fall as a breach in that unity. Your answer will depend on your personal opinion of Lady Dedlock and on your thoroughly analysing her character. You should also be aware of Dickens's evasive treatment of female sexuality.

Part 5

Suggestions for further reading

The text

The text used in writing these notes is the Penguin edition of *Bleak House*, Penguin Books, Harmondsworth, 1971. This is based on the 1853 edition and on the 1868 Charles Dickens Edition, which includes the author's final revisions.

Other works by Dickens

In 'Life of Charles Dickens' in the Introduction to these notes (pp. 5–8) you will find Dickens's other major works listed. You should read as many as possible in order to learn more about your author. *Pickwick Papers, Oliver Twist, David Copperfield* and *Great Expectations* might be suitable to start with; they are still popular novels, entertaining and not difficult.

If you want to know more about Dickens as a social critic, you should read *Dombey and Son* (1848) and above all *Little Dorrit* (1857). You will find it fascinating to discover on your own how Dickens managed to maintain a complete unity of theme with ever increasing skill and how he centred attacks around fraudulent companies or institutions (the Company of Dombey and Son, the Court of Chancery, the Circumlocution Office in *Little Dorrit*).

If you want to set *Bleak House* against a much wider social and literary background, you should read Balzac's *Le Père Goriot* (1835) and Dostoevsky's *The Brothers Karamazov* (1879–80). Both authors investigated their society in the same manner, by creating disturbing characters, by interdependence of plots and by inventing similar symbols of the moral decline of society.

Biography

The two full-scale biographies are:

FORSTER, JOHN: *The Life of Charles Dickens*, Hazell, Watson and Viney, London, 1872–4. An Edition (edited by J. W. T. Ley) was published by Doubleday, New York, 1928. John Forster was one of Dickens's closest friends and advisers.

JOHNSON, EDGAR: *The Life of Charles Dickens, His Tragedy and Triumph*, Gollancz, London, 1953.
For the 1970 Dickens centenary two pictorial biographies with critical studies were published. Their illustrations help to give an idea what life was like in Dickens's time:
PRIESTLEY, J. B.: *Charles Dickens and his World*, Thames and Hudson, London, 1970.
WILSON, ANGUS: *The World of Charles Dickens*, Secker & Warburg, London, 1970. This is the better of these two works; it contains a critical discussion of *Bleak House*.

General critical studies

All the following contain ciritical work on *Bleak House*:
BUTT, JOHN, and TILLOTSON, KATHLEEN: *Dickens at Work*, Methuen, London, 1957.
CAREY, JOHN: *The Violent Effigy, A Study of Dickens's Imagination*, Faber, London, 1973.
COLLINS, PHILIP: *Dickens and Crime*, (Papermac no. 134) Macmillan, London, 1965.
COLLINS, PHILIP (ed.): *Dickens, The Critical Heritage*, Routledge and Kegan Paul, London, 1971.
CONNOR, STEVEN: *Charles Dickens*, (Rereading Literature series, Basil Blackwell, Oxford, 1986.)
DALESKI, H. M.: *Dickens and the Art of Analogy*, Faber and Faber, London, 1970.
FIELDING, K. J.: *Charles Dickens: A Critical Introduction*, Longmans, London, 1970.
HOUSE, HUMPHREY: *The Dickens World*, (Oxford Paperbacks) Oxford University Press, London, 1972.
LEAVIS, F. R. and LEAVIS, Q. D.: *Dickens the Novelist*, Chatto and Windus, London, 1970. Contains an excellent analysis of *Bleak House*.
MILLER, J. HILLIS: *Charles Dickens: The World of his Novels*, Oxford University Press, London, 1958. A thorough analysis of *Bleak House* is included.
MONOD, SYLVÈRE: *Dickens the Novelist*, University of Oklahoma Press, Norman, Oklahoma, 1968.
ORWELL, GEORGE: 'Charles Dickens', in *Collected Essays*, Vol. 1, Secker and Warburg, London, 1968. A stimulating general essay on Dickens.

Critical essays on *Bleak House*

FORD, GEORGE and MONOD, SYLVÈRE (eds.): *Charles Dickens, Bleak House*, Norton Critical Edition, New York, 1977. Offers outstanding essays on the novel, together with an excellent selection of background material.

DYSON, A. E.: *Dickens: Bleak House: A Casebook*, Macmillan, London, 1977.

The following essays specifically deal with Esther's part in the novel:

AXTON, WILLIAM: 'The Trouble with Esther', in *Modern Language Quarterly*, 1965, pp. 545–57.

DYSON, A. E.: '*Bleak House:* Esther better not born?', in his *Casebook* (see above).

HARVEY, W. J.: 'The Double Narrative of *Bleak House*', in his *Character and the Novel*, Cornell University Press, Cornell, New York, 1965; also included with the Norton Critical Edition, (see above).

MONOD, SYLVÈRE: 'Esther Summerson, Charles Dickens and the Reader of *Bleak House*', in *Dickens Studies*, 1969, pp. 5–24.

General information

HARDWICK, MICHAEL and MOLLIE: *Charles Dickens Encyclopedia*, Omega Paperback, Futura Publications, London, 1973. This includes a complete catalogue of all Dickens's characters and gives an inventory of the places and buildings featured in his writings.

The author of these notes

J. J. Simon was educated at the Sorbonne and at the universities of Munich and Exeter. He now teaches at the Lycée Classique, Echternach, and at the Centre Universitaire. Luxembourg. He is the author of York Notes on Laurence Sterne's *Tristram Shandy*.